RESCUED

A HELEN MCPHEE COZY MYSTERY
BOOK 3

Liz Turner

Contents

Prologue
Raining Gunfire

The powerful beam of a flashlight flashed by. A man dove to the ground, holding in the grunt that formed as it knocked the air out of his lungs. He silently prayed that the roving lights did not catch the tip of his boot as it disappeared behind the rock.

His heart did not seem to beat anymore. Rather than regular, individual thumps, which offered the comforting reassurance that he was still alive and had not succumbed to a bullet in his back, his heart reverberated in his chest in a steady, endless ring of panic.

"I saw him!" echoed a harsh whisper. "There!" the hate-filled voice spat.

Whatever remaining sliver of hope the man had been clinging to drained pitifully into the base of his stomach and radiated waves of nausea. Seconds later, the first bullet chipped at the vibrating rock that served as the only shield between him and his pursuers. He held still, weathering the rattle of bullets that fired his way.

He took a deep breath and forced the terror out of his mind for the briefest of seconds, allowing the glimpse of a plan to form.

It was insane.

Absolutely ridiculous.

So insane and ridiculous that it might just work.

He grimaced with defiant hope at the surrounding darkness, his hand darting into his coat and pulling out a small flashlight. He stared at it, wondering if it would be enough.

There was a pause in the downpour of bullets. Men were likely reloading or scanning the area with their spotlights to determine if they had hit their target.

He took advantage of the respite, hurling his thick coat, which he had wormed out of with great difficulty, up and into the air, the glowing light hooked to the cuff of his coat sleeve.

The response was instant, and bullets rained down on the coat as it dropped to the ground. The man grunted loudly, feigning dying pain. This was not too hard to do since he had had many brushes with death.

"We've got him!" came the triumphant shout, followed by a few rumbled cheers.

As predicted, the men ceased fire, and a hundred beams highlighted the heap of a body covered by a thick winter coat.

He did not have long.

He seized every ounce of courage he had, dashed out from behind the fragment of rock that would not have protected him much longer, and ran as silently as he could through the open field.

He could see the darker shadow of the tree line looming into view ahead, so close.

Then men's voices sounded clearer, and he could hear the thump of their boots as they ran through the thick grass of the field. Their footsteps paused, and the man knew they had reached the empty coat. It would be seconds before—

"He's over there!" came a furious shout as they located his shadow sprinting for cover on a moonless night. He could tell it enraged them at having been deceived by such a pathetic ruse.

The man pushed forward, watching as blurred shapes of tree trunks formed out of the darkness of night. A few more steps and he would disappear into the forests he knew so well. He could not help grinning at the sweet taste of freedom when a single bullet wrenched the smile from his face.

He took mental stock. His legs kept carrying him forward, his lungs kept filling with oxygen, and his heart kept whirring along without missing a beat. He mentally located the source of the pain and blocked it out of his mind, forcing himself forward until he was in between the safety of thousands of ancient trees who would welcome him under their protective canopy.

Another bullet whizzed past his ear and shattered part of a tree trunk just ahead of him. The man immediately changed direction, grinning from ear to ear as the bullets fired further and further off target until they were a distant crack in the icy night air.

Chapter 1
The Lonely Hiker

"Gosh, I hate maps," Helen complained for the hundredth time, turning the leather-bound book upside down.

She tilted her head to the right to study the hiking trail sign, and back to the left where she tried to find the corresponding label on her map.

"He should've known I'd be useless with maps," she sighed.

She stared at the fork in the hiking trail. Both looked equally used, so her theory of taking the more worn path did not work. She glared at the faded signs, each pointing to a separate town but not indicating how far each town was away. She sighed heavily and dropped her eyes to the frustrating map. This time, she noticed a tiny handwritten note in the corner of the printed map.

For a Helen-friendly map, turn the page.

"So, he knew I was useless with maps," Helen chuckled, though her laugh caught in her throat.

Helen obeyed her dead husband's wishes and flipped the page, where she found a hand-drawn map painted in watercolors and labeled neatly in his own hand. Her husband had known her well. He had even drawn a stick figure carrying an enormous backpack and labeled it, *'You are here'*.

"Right," Helen nodded. "I've got that far already."

She studied her husband's map further. Peter had painted a bright red circle around Yellowwood Corner and included a giant yellow arrow, showing that this was where she would stay overnight.

"Thank you," she breathed, the words meant for her husband, wishing with all her might that he was alive to hear them.

She shifted the weight of her pack and felt the breeze cool the sweat on her back. It had been a long six miles with far more inclines than she was used to. The view at the top however had not only made her crawl along the trail because of her newfound fear of heights, but also gasp for air. She beheld glassy rivers weaving between spring green meadows and the dense green foliage of a certain tree, she now gathered were Yellowwood trees.

She had lain on the edge of the cliff trying to spot where she and Peter would have built their cottage, had they happened upon the land a decade ago, when they were still a fresh, young, married couple. Helen had decided the edge of the river would be best.

It would be cold, but they would have a wood stove which would constantly chug wisps of smoke into the air. Peter would fish and she would tame wild bears and foxes.

That was when Helen realized it could never be. And not just because her husband had died. She would never live in the same proximity as grizzly bears.

It was why she resolutely preferred the city. A mugger or some other psycho, which she could attempt to reason with might accost her, but there would be no wild animals involved. How could one reason with a bear?

Of course, the locals of Eldenbourg had assured Helen that their country was not home to wild animals like bears, lions, and wolves, but, then again, you could never trust a foreign country. They had also claimed that the tap water was safe and two days on a toilet had taught her otherwise.

"Excuse me," a voice penetrated her thoughts.

Helen jerked her head up and spun round. She realized, with growing humiliation, that she had been staring at her husband's map, her nose inches from the page, without moving for an immeasurable amount of time.

"Sorry," Helen mumbled, her cheeks red with fluster, "I sort of zoned out."

Before her stood a tall man with wild brown hair and an even wilder smile. He was in a ripped hiking jacket and carried no pack. His boots were muddied, and he looked as though he had been doing the real thing and staying in a tent, instead of the more decadent option of staying in a quaint village overnight, as Helen had chosen.

"I didn't mean to bother you," the man apologized, his voice raspy. "It's just that I had a bit of an accident," he said with a helpless shrug.

"What kind of accident?" Helen asked vaguely, while eyeing the tattoo of a swallow which poked out from under the cuff of his jacket.

"I lost my footing on one of the mountain trails. I scraped all the way down the front of the cliff and lost my pack."

Helen gasped in shock, snapping her notebook shut and feeling instantly horrid for not paying the suffering man more attention. She noticed that the untattooed hand was bleeding and covered in a filthy bandage which looked as though it may have been a sock. The sockless foot tucked into his boot confirmed her fear.

Her eyes whipped back to the man's eyes, and she noticed his pupils were not quite focused on her and his face was as white as snow.

"Sorry," he apologized, his hands reaching out blindly in front of him, his filthy hand grabbing her arm, "but I think I'm going to—"

The man crumpled to a heap at her feet. She assumed he was going to say 'faint' because that was exactly what he did. Helen glanced around in panic, hoping in vain that a group of hikers would pass along to assist her.

"What to do..." Helen mumbled to herself as she lowered her own heavy pack to the ground.

She thought of the time Peter had fallen off the roof while fixing some loose shingles. She had nursed him for days until he was well again.

Smiling fondly at the memory which helped to calm her, Helen unzipped her pack and pulled out the first aid kit her lawyer's assistant had so kindly packed for her. She opened it up and examined the contents for the first time.

Apart from a few blisters, Helen had managed her first real cross-country hike relatively unscathed.

She poured some of her drinking water into a bowl and used a cloth to clean up his hand. There was a giant hole between his right forefinger and thumb.

Even though blood usually turned her stomach, Helen pulled out a suture kit. She had patched up a few wounds in her time and was shocked to find that even though her brain had forgotten most of what to do, her fingers could still remember.

She sterilized the wound. The scorching pain of antiseptic against bare flesh woke the man who gurgled noisily with pain.

"What in the hell are you doing to me, woman!" he woke up yelling.

"Easy," she said, placing a hand on his chest. "Just lay back."

"It's nothing," he gasped, as she dabbed on more antiseptic.

"If we don't clean this of germs, and I'm not even going to mention the used sock you employed as a bandage, then you're going to develop an infection and lose your hand," she scolded him. "So, either you let me fix you up here, or you can wait another two hours for a nurse or a doctor to reach you from town. That's assuming another hiker stumbles across your unconscious body."

He stared at her with sunken eyes. He had clearly lost a lot of blood and was weakening the longer they left the wound open.

He nodded faintly, and Helen set to work. She stitched up the torn skin as best she could. Then she lathered it in ointment and patched it over with gauze and a bandage so that new dirt could not be introduced to the wound.

By the time she was done, she smiled at the man and noticed that he had passed out again, likely from the stabbing pain.

Helen took advantage, searching his exposed limbs for other injuries and cleaning any cuts she came across. He certainly looked like he had slid down a mountain, but even that did not explain the odd hole in his hand, unless he was as equally clumsy with his tent pegs and a mallet as he was with walking a steep trail.

By the time the man jerked back to consciousness, he was covered in band aids, and Helen had a happy little fire crackling near his feet and boiling some water for coffee.

He backed away from her as though she was the grizzly bear, but then seemed to realize she was the one who had helped him, and he slowly calmed down.

"Are you okay?" she asked gently, mildly perturbed by the man's strange behavior. "You've been asleep for a good hour."

He laughed, a grin reappearing on his pale face. "You know that sensation you have when you're asleep, but you feel you're falling? Mine was down a mountain again."

She giggled. "Here."

She handed him a tin mug of coffee and a ham sandwich.

"I'm not the greatest cook, so I'm afraid the only food I have..." she paused, words evading her as she watched him shove the entire sandwich into his mouth. "How many days did you say you've been stuck out here?"

"Two," he managed in between monstrous chews. "There's only so many berries you can eat."

"Exactly!" Helen agreed with a laugh. "I was lost in these woods for a night last week and ended up living on berries. 'Blue is safe for you, red is dead,'" she recalled with fondness. "I know exactly the problems you have had to endure," she said, looking at his stomach and rubbing her own as the painful memory re-surged.

He chuckled. "How did you get lost? You seem so organized."

"Oh," she waved a hand, "apart from the fact that I am possibly the worst hiker in the world. I only agreed to do this hike because it was a holiday my late husband had planned for the pair of us before he…" Helen froze.

She rarely brought her husband into just any conversation. She was stunned that she had spoken of it so easily. "Anyway," Helen shook herself back to reality, "while staying in the previous village, poachers kidnapped me and after I escaped I had to survive for a night on my own."

The man stared at her, shock written all over his face.

"What did you say your name was?" he asked.

"Helen," she replied. "Helen McPhee. And yours?"

There it was again. The uncertainty that played across his face in split second increments.

"Gary," he answered with a smile. "You seem like quite the woman," he remarked.

"No," she shook her head. "I'm just a trouble magnet. In fact, you shouldn't hang around with me too long. The first grizzly in Eldenbourg will find us and decide we look edible."

"You do know there aren't any bears here?" he said with a laugh.

"But because it's me, there would be one," she said seriously. "Escaped from Africa, or something."

"Alright then." He regarded her suspiciously, as though he had stumbled over yet another crazy American tourist who believed his country was wrought with lions and that flush toilets did not exist. He was not even going to tackle the notion of grizzly bears escaping from Africa. "Anyway, I feel much better now and I should get on my way. Where are you heading?"

"Yellowwood Wood," she replied. "I think it's a town."

"Not quite. It's the name of the forest around the town you will stay in. It's because of all the Yellowwoods. You're looking for a small town called Ochre."

"Like the paint color?"

"I think so," he replied with a shrug. "I'm not much of an artist."

"Then why the bird?"

"Bird?"

She gestured to his wrist and watched as he quickly tugged his jacket sleeve down.

"It's just something to remind me never to give up hope that freedom is possible," he replied, his eyes a million miles away.

"Well," Helen said, packing away her things, "here is a small pack to get you to the next village, unless you're heading my way."

He shook his head quickly. "No, I'm heading in the opposite direction." He took the small bag and peered inside at the food and spare water bottle she had supplied him with. There was also a fresh pair of socks. He smiled gratefully.

"It was interesting meeting you, Gary," Helen said, while swinging her pack onto her back. "I doubt we will meet again, but I hope you find what you're looking for."

"Huh?" he shrugged gruffly.

"Freedom," she replied with a smile. "I hope you find the freedom you're looking for. Cheerio," she said with a wave and a backward glance over her shoulder. "Stay safe."

"Helen," he called over his shoulder, a smile rippling through his lips. "Thank you."

The man waited a good hour, concealing himself in the dense bush which skirted the narrow hiking trail. Then, when the sun was setting, and all the other hikers had already made their way to a village for the night, Gary selected the fork in the road Helen had, making his way slowly to Ochre.

Chapter 2
The Star of Ochre

Helen followed the few road signs leading to the town of Ochre. Eventually, she stumbled across a rundown farmhouse, which looked as though it only housed cats and ghosts. She stopped to ask for directions and was told that she was in Ochre. Well, on the very outskirts, but she had apparently arrived.

"And do other hikers stay here too?" Helen asked, trying to mask her dubiety.

She was informed, in a rather prissy tone, that she was standing in one of the most popular towns in the country of Eldenbourg, though, when Helen asked why the old farmer's wife could not think of a suitable reply. The crotchety woman assured Helen that she would find some of the best food and accommodation in the world.

Helen's face refused to hide her doubt and so the woman insisted that she find a man called Boris and stay at his backpacker's inn.

"Be sure to tell him that Olga sent you!" the woman insisted with a high-pitched cackle.

Helen thought the woman rather kind to provide a recommendation. She skipped along the rather overgrown trail and into what looked like a fairly poor excuse for a merry little European village, which had been promised in the travel brochures.

"I'm looking for Boris," Helen stated for the fourth time, her lips working hard to enunciate each word clearly so the woman, selling an assortment of wild herbs Helen had never laid eyes on, could hear her.

The woman with wild, grey eyebrows beheld Helen with a deathly pale face and pointed a trembling finger over Helen's shoulder. Once the smoke cleared from the burning herbs, which caused Helen to feel rather lightheaded, Helen glimpsed a rough stone cottage across the bumpy lane.

"Thank you," Helen said, before choking on more of the fragrant smoke and retreating with watery eyes and a resigned wave.

As she hopped across the muddy lane, her stomach growled in angry protest at having nothing but three ham sandwiches and several apples on a grueling eight-hour hike, Helen hurried as fast as her tired legs could carry her to the signboard which read: *The Star of Ochre.*

She glanced up at the pokey windows, which offered no insight into the enormous cottage with the straggly roof and weathered gargoyles ogling her from above. A shiver raked down her spine, and she reread the name for reassurance.

"If this is the star, I hate to see what the rest of the town looks like," she mumbled, more to herself than for the benefit of the other hikers she saw bustling around.

"What was that?" an eerie voice whined behind her.

Helen jumped round, her pack jangling as pots clanked against steel cups and stray knives and forks that had gone missing during the hike.

"Oh my goodness, you scared me half to death," Helen stammered with a nervous laugh. "I was just reading this sign and thought how intriguing it is."

The man spiked a shaggy eyebrow and stared at her over the rims of his circular spectacles.

"And are you interested in staying here for the night? We offer a most delicious chicken stew to our guests, paired with some home brewed ale and freshly baked bread."

"All very tempting," Helen said, forcing a smile, "but it all depends on whether or not you're Boris."

Helen watched as the middle-aged man's thin lips twisted into what she assumed was a smile.

"I am, indeed," he replied, much to her horror. He stroked a clammy hand down the front of his brown knitted jersey, which bore so many holes it could only pass for fashion on the most extreme of catwalks.

"Oh," Helen said, pausing as words escaped her. "And this is your establishment?" she asked while glancing at the grim building.

"It is quite cozy on the inside," he assured her with a toadlike smirk. "I accept all payments upfront. Shall we proceed to reception? We're almost fully booked, you see."

Despite appearances, which were ghastly, Boris was the epitome of a gentleman. She watched as he whipped a hand through his greasy wisp of hair and grinned at her, the gaps in his yellowed teeth almost comical.

"Alright," she agreed after taking a deep breath. "Olga recommended you, after all."

"Olga?" his head spun around, and he glared at her through narrow slits. "What did that old hag say about me?"

"Only that you offered some of the best accommodation in town," Helen explained, while backing away from him.

The oddly serene smile returned in an instant, and he gestured towards a heavy wrought iron door labeled 'reception', showing that she should lead the way.

Helen gulped, shifted the weight of her heavy pack on her back, and forced herself forward despite her gut telling her to run in the opposite direction. She pulled open the door to reception and almost held her breath in anticipation.

To her surprise, the room was relatively pleasant. There was a little fireplace in the corner, casting a warm glow across the cramped space. An old rug was strewn over the roughly hewn stone floor, and they nestled a red velvet armchair close to the fireplace for any tired hiker waiting to make payment for their bed.

Boris pushed past her, his chest briefly brushing against her arm as he did. She heaved the pack off her back and resisted the urge to drop into the dusty armchair and order a cheeseburger.

"Right, so one night or two?" Boris inquired politely, his hand poised over the register.

"I usually stay a few nights in each town," Helen explained, "because I'm not exactly a fit hiker and it often takes a while before my joints move again," she added with a laugh.

Boris cleared his throat and continued to stare at her.

"Let's say two nights," she replied quickly.

A rather haggard-looking cat leapt up onto the armchair, scaring Helen half to death. After she had gotten over her initial fright, Helen cooed affectionately at it and reached out an eager hand to pet it. The feline hissed at her and slapped a clawed paw against Helen's hand, leaving four hairline slashes in her skin.

"Ouch! You dirty little beast!" Helen cried while recoiling from the cat.

"That's Agatha," Boris informed her. "She keeps an eye on things. Makes sure none of the guests steal."

Helen eyed the cat with growing suspicion. The abominable creature was hairless in some patches.

"What does it do if it catches a thief?" Helen asked fearfully. She kept a wary eye on the feral being, which was pointedly circling the armchair and emitting a low rumble of disapproval from her chest.

Boris smiled again, though this time it was as creepy as the green glare radiating from Agatha.

"Right, all you have to do is sign here," Boris said, turning the book to her. "And hand over the fee."

Helen nearly gasped at the fee. It was one of the most expensive places she had stayed in since her journey across Eldenbourg had begun, but Boris did not seem to joke. She handed over her precious dollars, reminding herself that her husband had left her a small fortune in his will, and being stingy got no one anywhere in life.

Besides, there was the promised chicken stew to look forward to.

"Would you like to proceed to the bunk room, or to the dining room?"

"Definitely food," Helen gushed with relief that she could eat soon.

The cat meowed ferociously as Helen attempted to move past it.

"There, there," Boris soothed his prickly cat. "This woman is a guest now. So be sure to keep an eye on her."

"Excuse me," Helen complained, feeling annoyance ripple through her. "I am no thief."

"That's what they all say," Boris replied with an eye roll.

Helen could not be certain, but as the slovenly man shoved past her yet again, she had the odd sensation that his gentlemanly manner had died the moment she handed him her money.

"This way," he grumbled, pushing through a narrow door which her pack scraped on both sides.

She hurried to follow him and after a long, winding passage, in which she bumped her head on low hanging lights several times, she ended up in a dimly lit dining room which smelled terribly of damp and as though something had died.

Helen seated herself at one of the many empty tables and immediately felt as though she had a hundred eyes on her, despite not being able to see any of the other diners. Something hard slinked against her leg and she realized Agatha was doing her job frisking her for stolen goods.

"Shoo," Helen moaned at the cat under the table. "I will not enjoy my meal with you watching every mouthful."

Helen felt a presence and sat upright, finding Boris staring down his pudgy nose at her.

"I'd prefer it if you refrained from harassing my cat," he said with a sneer sweeping across his lips. "Dinner is served," he added, setting the bowl down in front of her.

Helen realized the smell she had encountered upon entering the dining room was, in fact, coming from the food itself. Something had died in the kitchen, and it had been cooked and served up as dinner. The question which raided her mind of sanity was, how long had the unidentifiable animal been dead?

She glanced at the watery stew which had several unrecognizable vegetables floating around in it and no chicken in sight, unless that was what the shapeless, grey blobs were supposed to be. She forced back a gag, and simpered faintly, eagerly watching the loaf of bread as he set it down next to the bowl. At least she could stuff herself full on bread and the promised ale.

"And your drink," Boris concluded, setting the dented pitcher down. He then disappeared promptly, so that she could make no complaints or suggestions.

Helen pushed the stew away and grabbed the bread. She spent five minutes trying to wrest a piece off the solid rock which could likely kill Agatha, if the opportunity presented itself. Crunching on the dry bread, she nearly choked as it stuck in her throat, soaking up any saliva that could help guide it safely down her esophagus.

Grabbing the mug of 'home brewed ale', she chugged a few sips before realizing it was nothing more than watered-down ale, and she held the growing suspicion that the water used was likely drain water.

Utterly dissatisfied and fighting to suppress a raging stomach that thrashed at her with savage hunger, Helen forced the meal away from her. She looked up and saw Boris watching her through a crack in the door. Mortified, she drew the ale back to her and stomached another sip before pulling up from the table.

Boris was at her side again.

"I'm afraid I'm not as hungry as I thought I was," she explained, while he was eyeing her full bowl. "Perhaps I just need to get to the room and settle in."

He raised an eyebrow but said nothing. He twitched his head toward yet another door and walked away. Helen followed, lugging her pack behind her.

The gentleman was gone.

Chapter 3
Rats & Beer

The bunkroom had been dingy, damp, and cold, but the mattresses looked semi-decent. Helen reasoned she had her own sleeping bag to shield her from any of the unseen germs lurking in the less than clean hovel, and so she decided not to make any further complaints.

She was all ready to accept her fate for the evening when something light passed over the toe of her boot. She glanced down and found an enormous, greasy rat sitting next to her foot, nibbling on what looked like a chunk of bread from dinner.

Despite all the screaming and the fact that Helen exited the room by leaping from bed to bed, Boris did not reappear to check on the concerns of his newest guest. And even when she had decided to give him a piece of her mind, he was nowhere to be found.

And so, Helen took matters into her own hands. She braved the rat-infested bunkroom, strapped her pack on her back, and marched out hoping to find entirely new accommodations and a decent meal to calm the beast, which was ready to murder any innocent bystander who crossed her path.

As she was leaving the cottage, she felt the odd sensation of being watched. She spun around and examined the dull grey walls of the cottage, but she saw only the flash of dark fabric disappearing behind a hedge and nothing more.

Once on the streets of Ochre again, with her heavy pack getting heavier with each step, Helen convinced herself that the village was not all bad. At least three people had smiled at her, and some of the evening shops had little lanterns hanging in the window to give them an almost cheery appearance.

The town clock gonged and suddenly there was a lot more foot traffic all around her, as though everyone in the village had abruptly taken to the streets. The only thing stranger than this was that they dressed all the men up as scarecrows. It was not Halloween, and could not be Guy Fawkes either, because the date was wrong, but she assumed it had something to do with a local harvest festival.

Kids were handing out paper cups filled with salty popcorn and women weaved garlands out of wheat, which they wore around their heads. She accepted one with a smile and even skipped to the beat of a local band as they warmed up their instruments for the evening.

As Helen walked between the gurgle of cheerful voices and laughing children, she felt that her stay in Ochre would not be so bad after all.

That was, until she saw the lines for the food stalls. She had to wait almost half an hour to get to the front of the queue, but the corn wraps filled with steak, corn, cheese, and a fresh salad were well worth the wait.

She also purchased plenty of real beer to make up for the awful encounter she had experienced in Boris's dining room.

By the end of the evening, Helen had almost forgotten the unpleasant start to the unorthodox village of Ochre, and she even dropped her pack to sing and dance with the merrier party makers, who had likely consumed as much beer as she had.

As Helen looked around at the laughing, rosy-cheeked faces, she almost forgot that she was alone and had lost the love of her life. Despite the aching pain which usually plagued every waking moment of her life, Helen felt like she could laugh again, dance again, and smile again, without as much guilt as she had felt before. More than that, she felt something new entering her heart.

Peace.

Or at least the hope that after many long years, she could find peace without her husband at her side.

She finished her beer and decided it was time for bed. She slipped away from the crowd, content that she had at least taken part in something new and exciting. She pushed from her mind the urge to run home and tell a waiting Peter all about it.

Instead, she contented herself to conclude that the street festival was something Peter would have loved, and he had been right to plan their holiday there, despite her initial reservations.

"I'm afraid we're fully booked. Try next door," the man said with a concerned smile.

Next door was full too.

"We rarely have guests requesting accommodation this late," came the anxious reply of a third backpacker's inn. "We're all full up here!"

"I'm afraid we've even had to rent out our own bedroom," came another apologetic response. "It is the harvest festival, you know. There won't be an empty bed, or a free patch of grass to pitch a tent, for miles. Unless..." the woman hesitated, her eyes flicking to her husband's, as if to request confirmation to proceed.

The man raised his eyebrows and shook his head vehemently.

"Where else will she go?" the woman muttered.

"Anywhere but there!" the husband hissed.

The wife sighed. "There's one last option. Have you tried the Star of Ochre?" she continued gravely. "Boris always has spare beds."

Helen accepted this with as much dignity as she could muster. She did not explain that she had abandoned her booking with Boris to seek something more decent and now, as the streets emptied and the drunken singing faded, she had to return to the dark cottage with the horrible gargoyles and hope Boris and his friend would not notice.

But he did.

As Helen tried to sneak back in, Agatha sounded the siren with a shrill shriek and Boris leapt up from the red armchair with a club in his hand.

"It's just me," Helen said, hands raised. "I was just out at the festival. Sorry to get back so late."

Boris scowled at her, his eyes absorbing the hiking pack on her back. He surveyed her for a moment, as if working out her coy little plan and the failed attempt to find alternative accommodation.

"One night or two," he said loudly, flipping his register open.

"What do you mean?" Helen snapped. "I've already paid for two nights."

"But you left, forfeiting your booking," he stated confidently while pointing his pen at her pack. "You had no intention of sleeping here, but since you couldn't find anywhere else, you've returned and clearly desperately need lodgings. One night or two?" he repeated without the slightest ounce of shame.

"I'm not paying you again!" she complained. "Your food is absolutely atrocious, you water your ale down, and your bread is at least a week old. Apart from that," she gathered stamina from the remaining festival beer pumping through her system, "a rat in the bunkroom accosted me!"

"Why didn't you say anything?" he asked slowly. "Had you complained, I may have been able to attend to you, but since you left without so much as a single word, I cannot refund you. I'm asking you for the last time before I turn you out onto the street, one night?"

She scowled at him and chewed on her lip while she silently weighed up her options, of which she only had one.

"One blasted night," Helen conceded between gritted teeth, knowing full well there were more rats on the streets than in Boris's house.

She forked out a handful of dollars and ignored the smug smirk that proudly displayed itself on Boris's flushed face.

Helen heaved up her pack and stomped her heavy hiking boots all the way to the chilly bunk room which housed another twelve unfortunate hikers, who had encountered the same misfortune as she had: being stuck at Boris's star of Ochre.

Helen dumped her pack on a bunk and slumped down next to it to pull off her heavy hiking boots. The mattress springs squealed in protest, and she swore a cloud of dust lifted from the hessian blanket. She flexed each foot and gave it a rub till she felt she could bear hobbling barefoot to the shower.

A couple of weeks of hiking had taken a toll on her body. She had slowly developed muscles in her arms and legs, and while her back was still exhausted, it was not broken as she'd feared when she first embarked on her journey across Eldenbourg.

Helen set up her sleeping bag for the night and gathered her towel and pajamas, the famous yellow duck ones which had caused her considerable trouble along the way, and started walking towards the bathroom, which not only smelled dank and moldy but which seemed to house a polar wind.

After a lukewarm shower, Helen dressed as quickly as she could and bolted to her bed, where she discovered a man rifling through her pack.

"Excuse me," she interrupted him.

He looked up at her with a vague, disinterested expression and withdrew his hand.

"There was a rat inside," he explained.

Helen almost believed him, but then she saw Agatha was pacing the room and she knew that if there had really been a rat, the lethal cat would have sprung into action. A glance at her bag confirmed this, for she noticed that the position of her money pouch had shifted, and she knew the undercover thug was making an excuse for being caught mid robbery.

"How kind of you to get rid of the critter," Helen said. "My name is Helen."

"I'm Luke," he replied, his pale blue eyes flickering away from her as though he was contemplating how to escape his conversation with her.

"And what do you think of Ochre?"

He shrugged and ran a hand through his mess of blonde curls. "I don't really care much for it."

Helen nodded, running out of discussion points. Her family lawyer, Alex, had encouraged her to use the journey to make friends again.

Since her husband had died, she had developed the tendency to withdraw and cocoon herself in her bed for weeks on end, or plan imaginary friendships with the fictional characters she met in the series she binge-watched. But her odd encounter with Luke, where he was not only trying to steal from her but also seemed to make no attempt to return her polite conversation, was enough to make her retreat with gratitude to her hermit ways.

Helen watched as Luke drifted to a bunk bed close to hers. He pulled a rucksack onto the bed and pulled out a small flask, which he unscrewed and guzzled. Her nose prickled at the sharp twang of spirits in the air.

Helen noticed Luke had no hiker's pack, or boots lying around. Instead of the usual sleeping bag, he was using the linin Boris provided. Luke waved the flask in her direction, clearly offering her a sip, but she smiled politely and shook her head.

"I've had a little too much beer already," she giggled. "I needed something to wash down the awful ale Boris served here."

To her surprise, Luke cracked a delayed smile.

"I thought I was going to barf when he set the pork stew in front of me," Luke explained.

"That wasn't pork," she said with a laugh. "It was supposed to be chicken."

The young man laughed, and his face paled even more. "Oh, hell no! I had three spoonfuls. No wonder I don't feel so good."

There was an uncomfortable screech and Agatha leapt onto Helen's bed, her patches of fur standing on end.

"It's as though she knows we're bad-mouthing her owner," Helen whispered to Luke, who had gotten a fright from the cat. He opened his flask again and took a long swig.

"Boris said he was leaving Agatha here to keep the rats away," Luke explained, when his nerves had finally settled. "Though I think she's hunting us more than the rats."

Helen had to use her smaller backpack to shoo the hissing cat off her bed so that she could slip into her sleeping back and not have her throat slashed by a cat assassin.

"Are you heading out on a hike early in the morning?" Helen asked obscurely, still curious why Luke was staying at Boris.

Luke glowered immediately, and he nodded. "Something like that. Though I may stick around for a few days. Anyway, night."

He flicked off the light closest to his bed, casting their corner of the bunk room into darkness.

"Night," Helen whispered, secretly relieved that she was not alone in the awful cottage with the even more awful cat.

As she lay in the musky room staring up at the ceiling and feeling the air turn to ice around her ears, she could hear the click of Agatha's permanently extended claws ticking against the stone floor.

It was going to be a long night.

Chapter 4
Snuggling Cats & Dead Roommates

Helen stretched in her sleeping bag, the ends of her toes pushing against the outer zip that trapped her inside. She rolled onto her back, content that despite the horrendous place she was staying in, she had enjoyed a decent night's sleep.

And then something else moved inside her sleeping bag.

Helen's eyes snapped open, and she froze while her groggy mind tried to decipher if what she had felt had been part of her conscious reality or not. She felt two long arms stretch up onto her chest. Claws appeared which pricked through the yellow duck fabric of her pajamas, contacting her skin before retracting again.

"Oh no," Helen breathed. "This can't be happening."

She tried to adjust, without disturbing the four-legged creature that had snuck into her sleeping bag in the middle of the night, but it was impossible. Agatha caught wind that her heat host was awake and so she forced her way out of the narrow opening of the sleeping bag, flicking her tail in Helen's face as she turned to hop off the bed.

Helen sat upright and immediately began scratching all over, her skin blotching red wherever she had contacted Agatha's flea-infested fur. She yawned and decided she would have to brave the ice-cold showers again before beginning her day. That was when she realized that all the other hikers had already left, being sure to skip breakfast so they could avoid Boris's cooking.

Helen saw one bed was still occupied. Luke was still asleep. But oddly, he was not alone. A tall, hulking figure in a brown, holey sweater was standing over Luke, his hands submerged in the depths of Luke's rucksack.

"What are you doing?" Helen asked loudly.

Boris's head snapped up and his eyes found her. He panicked for a moment, frozen with his hands still stuck inside Luke's bag, but then he wrenched them out, money notes jammed between his clammy fingers.

"You're stealing!" Helen shrieked while fighting to get out of her sleeping bag.

Agatha was howling, determined to defend her beloved owner to the best of her ability. The feline inserted herself in Helen's direct path to Boris, where she lashed out sharp claws at Helen every time she took a step forward.

Boris used the opportunity to escape. His fingers still crunched round the notes he had stolen from Luke's bag.

"Luke!" Helen screamed. "You're being robbed!"

Boris had disappeared behind a dusty tapestry hanging on the wall. When Helen pulled the ancient rug away, she found nothing but a stone wall, as though Boris had disappeared down some kind of trap door to a concealed passage. Helen was studying the various stones for one which stood out when something in her mind prodded at her with increasing urgency.

She turned slowly, realizing Luke had never responded to her shouts, which had been loud enough to wake the dead.

"Luke?" she repeated, while her bare feet carried her tentatively closer to the steel frame of his bunk bed where he lay perfectly still.

There was no response. As she neared him, she glimpsed his deathly pale face, which looked as though it was covered in a thin layer of ice. His lips were tinged blue, and she wondered if he had frozen in the night.

"Luke," she said loudly, annoyed by the uncertain wobble in her own voice. Her feet were numb against the frosty touch of the stone floor.

There was still no response.

Helen noticed that Luke's chest was as still as the rest of his body. Helen closed the last step between them and held a trembling finger under his nose to feel for the movement of his breath. She could not feel the warm air push out his nose and blow against her skin, and it was only when her hand accidentally brushed against his top lip and she felt the ice-cold touch of his skin that she threw herself backward in horror and screamed for help.

Luke was undeniably dead.

Helen had propped herself up in the furthest corner of the bunkroom, her sweaty hand clutching a bottle of pepper spray and her eyes still fixed on Luke's unmoving body. She had not dared to leave, in case the grave-robbing Boris returned to finish the job.

She had jumped at every scratch of a rat or hiss of Boris's awful cat, but despite all this, her courage was intact enough for her to wait out the police. After what felt like hours since her call with Officer Noah Wolff, Helen heard footsteps descending into the musty bunkroom.

She turned and aimed her pepper spray at the base of the stairs on the off chance that the newcomer was not her trusted friend, Noah.

Which it was not.

Instead of Noah, another uniformed officer walked in, his shiny shoes clipping smartly against the floor. His slick light blonde hair was in stark contrast to the dark navy blue of his uniform. He wore his uniform with pride, each bronze button carefully polished in the weak morning light that filtered through the overgrown windows. She watched as his dark eyes carefully surveyed the room before snapping onto hers.

"Good morning," he greeted, a smile radiating out of every inch of his face.

Helen back away, her head bumping into a jutted stone in the wall.

"It's alright. I'm with the police. I heard a woman discovered the body. Are you her?"

Helen nodded, her hand slowly relaxing on the trigger of the pepper spray.

"Where's Officer Wolff?" Helen asked. "I called his station."

"I don't know where he is. All I know is that a call was made at the station about a dead body, and I was obviously the closest officer on hand," he explained. "I'm Officer Rosco

Oliveira," he continued while approaching her with a warm smile.

Helen remained silent. Her eyes flicked from the official-looking police badge to the gold cufflink on his outstretched hand.

"It's alright," he assured her in a voice that soothed her frazzled nerves. "I'm here to help, I promise."

Helen slowly lowered her armed pepper spray and forced a glum smile.

"My name's Helen McPhee, and I was the one to discover the body this morning," she explained. "I was the one who made the call, too."

"And you stayed with the body the whole time?" he asked, a little surprised.

Helen nodded.

"That was very brave of you," he offered gently, and in a manner that did not seek to condescend to her.

"His name is Luke," Helen continued, gaining confidence. "We met last night before bed. I don't think he was a serious hiker because he didn't have a pack. He also seemed really depressed about something."

"Why would you say that?" officer Oliveira asked, more out of intrigue than anything else.

Helen approached the body cautiously.

"He kept drinking from a flask of alcohol. It seemed to steady his nerves. He only had a small bag, so I think he was just here for the night," Helen continued. "Though he tried to give the impression that he was a hiker like me."

"Did he say anything about his business in Ochre?" Rosco inquired while making notes in his little book, his dark eyes flashing around the room like an eagle's.

"No," Helen replied.

"Then it's all speculation," Rosco replied dismissively.

"Hardly," Helen scoffed. "I think Luke was up to something. This morning I awoke to the owner of this backpacker's inn searching through Luke's bag and he seemed to have tons of cash."

"What?" Rosco spun around on his heel, ignoring the part about the cash. "Who is this owner?"

"His name is Boris, and he's shocking. I didn't see him harming Luke, but he certainly took his time going through Luke's things," Helen explained. "That was, until I awoke and caught him in the act."

"And where is Boris now?"

Helen shrugged. "I haven't seen him. I was too scared to leave the body in case Boris returned to cover his tracks."

"Clever thinking," the man acknowledged with an impressed smirk. "You've certainly got a brain on you."

Rosco began poking around in Luke's backpack when another set of feet traveled down the stone staircase and into the dingy bunkroom.

"Helen?" sounded a familiar voice.

Noah Wolff stepped into the room with his partner, Ruby Taylor, behind him.

"Are you alright?" Noah asked, hurrying over to her the second his eyes found her. "When I heard an American had put the call through, I was sure it was you."

Even Ruby held a flicker of concern in her ocean blue eyes set in a porcelain face.

"I'm fine," Helen assured them. "Really. Whatever happened, I slept through it."

"Wolff," Rosco said with an air of something Helen could not quite put her finger on.

"Rosco," Noah stammered uncertainly. "Why are you -"

"What are you doing here, Oliveira?" Ruby blurted, the annoyance clear in her voice.

Helen backed out from between the three officers. It was the first time she had ever heard Ruby direct her irritation at anyone other than Helen herself. Though, Ruby's disposition towards Helen had changed drastically after they had saved each other's lives in the previous town.

"I responded to the call at the station," Rosco replied mildly. "I thought I could help."

Ruby folded her muscular arms across her chest. "You know perfectly well that this is our jurisdiction. We don't need your help here."

Rosco glared at her. He was unshaken by Ruby's runway figure and model petulance, which usually had other men speaking in monosyllabic words when she accosted them.

"Look," Rosco held up his hands in surrender and smiled, "I assure you I'm not here to step on any toes, especially not a partnership as renowned as yours. But I am working another case and so that brings me into your territory."

Noah stepped forward and extended a peace offering with a handshake. "I'm sure we can all get along just fine."

"So, you're letting him walk all over our case, just like that?" Ruby retorted. "He's just going to get in the way."

Helen watched Rosco to see his reaction, but he kept a tight rein on his temper. He seemed to have the superhuman ability not to allow Ruby to get under his skin. Helen marveled at him.

"I'll try to stay out the way, and follow your lead," Rosco said, attempting to pacify her. "My only goal is to help."

Ruby looked like a terrier, ready to fight tooth and nail for her turf.

"Not to interrupt," Helen said with a croak in her voice, "but there is a dead body literally lying in the middle of all this, so the faster we get to the clues, the faster we may figure this all out."

"You're right, of course," Rosco said apologetically, his hand resting on the front of his chest. "Since you were here through the entire ordeal, Helen, can you provide us with any more details?"

"Apart from a brief conversation last night, and waking up to find Boris looting the body, not much. I slept like the dead last night, which is rather unusual. Although, if I'm honest," Helen colored, "I had had several beers the night before."

"I see," Noah nodded with a twitch of a smile. "So, you heard nothing in the night?"

"No, I'm afraid not. Can I ask," Helen chewed on a fingernail, her anxiety spiking as the question formed in her mind, "are you assuming that he died of natural causes or do you think someone..."

Helen dared not complete the sentence. A shiver worked its way down her spine at the thought of being in the same space as a murderer. As she wrapped her arms around her waist, she realized with horror that she was addressing these professional people while wearing her dreaded yellow duck pajamas. She flushed bright red.

Of course Noah and Ruby had rescued her twice before and had been witness to the ridiculous, orange-billed inspired pajamas, but the rather handsome Officer Oliveira with his impossible head of hair and dark eyes which seemed to see into her soul, let alone see through the thin fabric of the worst pajamas in the world.

She had packed them for comfort more than anything, believing that she would stay in a suite in a luxurious hotel, and not with a room full of ruffians at a backpacker's inn, paired with the humiliation of a communal bathroom. She had also never imagined that her journey to find herself again while crossing a country on foot would lead to so many criminal encounters.

Helen darted to her backpack, yanked out a set of clean clothes, and slipped away to the bathroom, allowing the police to do their policing thing. As she returned to the room, her duck pajamas creeping out from under the towel she had used to dry herself, there was a full-fledged argument underway.

"It must be strangulation," Rosco argued. "How can you not see it?"

"Based on what?" Ruby practically snarled. "Because he's not breathing?" she asked in a mocking tone, her strong jawline clenching while she waited for an answer.

"The color of his lips," Rosco pointed out. "They're blue. Someone clearly deprived him of air."

"He's right," Noah intervened. "I believe the coloring of his face shows they cut his oxygen supply off."

Helen shoved her things in her bag and shot a glance between the towering shoulders of Noah and Rosco, who had their backs to her. She spotted a glimpse of Luke's pale and exposed torso and neck.

"Ask her opinion," Ruby said loudly, a long arm pointing at Helen.

Helen jolted in fright. Ruby's innate hatred for Helen had usually escalated when Helen interrupted during a case, so Helen was used to observing quietly from the sidelines. She stared blankly at Ruby, uncertain of whether her invitation to speak was a trap.

"Helen has a good eye for detail," Ruby said gruffly. "If you're comfortable, Helen, I'd like you to look and tell us what you think the cause of death is."

Helen swallowed her surprise. Having saved each other's lives in the woods when poachers had been seconds away from pulling the trigger really brought even the worst of enemies together. Helen nearly choked on her own breath when Ruby offered a hesitant smile, as if to reassure Helen of her sincerity.

Helen returned the smile with uncertainty. She stepped up between the towering frames of the two officers and forced her eyes to study the unmoving figure lying on the bed.

"There are no marks on his neck." This was the first thing Helen noticed as she forced away the queasiness. She had binge-watched so many detective series during her shutdown after Peter died that she had witnessed a wide range of gory bodies on screen. She felt this in part qualified her to examine a body with a certain amount of expertise.

"Bruising can take several hours," Rosco corrected her.

"I also think if someone was strangling him, I would've heard something," Helen mumbled while continuing her study. "I agree with Noah about his lips. He definitely ran out of air. What about suffocation? That would explain the pillow on the floor next to his bed."

The three officers stepped back as though they had not noticed the floor, while Helen stepped forward, her nose picking up a peculiar smell. Her bare foot stuck to something on the floor as she stepped closer and she jumped away, her back bumping into Officer Oliveira's chest.

"Sorry!" she babbled as his hands caught and held her upright.

Helen did not hear his reply because she was focused on the invisible droplets of something sticky on the floor next to Luke's bed. She stooped and slowly lowered her head to the drops, drawing away as a faint, yet sickly sweet smell plunged up her nostrils.

"It smells worse than hospital disinfectant," she complained.

Noah dropped to his knees next to her, not giving a second thought to his pristine uniform that he had likely spent two hours a morning ironing. He gave the substance a sniff himself.

"You said that the man had been drinking last night," Rosco reminded them. "He probably just spilled something on the floor."

"Here's his flask," Ruby confirmed. "And it's still got some alcohol inside. Smells sweet enough. Maybe it's a match."

Helen and Noah both sniffed the bottle.

"Not the same," Noah shook his head. "I'll take a sample, but I can say with almost certainty that this is chloroform. It evaporates quickly, which could be why the scent is so faint."

"So, the victim was likely drugged while he was sleeping," Ruby stated. She stooped and gave Luke's lips and mouth a tentative sniff. She recoiled. "We will need to send a sample of this area of his face to the lab as well. Although the results will take a century to get all the way out here."

"I agree with Helen. He was likely suffocated with the pillow," Noah agreed. "I'm sure you can smell chloroform on the pillow, though it's too faint to tell."

"Hold up," Rosco chuckled, "before you all get ahead of yourselves. It takes a good fifteen minutes to make someone pass out using chloroform."

"What?" Helen gasped. "It takes seconds in the movies."

"I hope Hollywood is not the source of information you're basing all your observations on," Rosco fired at her with a twinkle in his eye.

Again, he had seen straight through her, in more than one sense. That was exactly the source of her information.

"That is true," Ruby agreed, "but the fact that he was already asleep and had had a lot to drink would have sped up the process. This way, the killer could take him out without a sound, as long as he was patient."

As all of this accumulated information dawned on Helen, she felt as though she was going to faint. It was not the empty anxious feeling of her stomach gnawing at her since breakfast was long overdue, but more the dreaded realization that a killer had potentially been standing a few feet from her, taking his sweet time to murder Luke, while she slept on peacefully.

"Are you alright?" Rosco asked, his eyes on her and his hand supporting her elbow as her body grew more and more slack. "Maybe you should sit down."

Helen allowed him to lead her to the bed, where she lowered herself unsteadily to the uncomfortable mattress. She could feel the icy film of cold sweat break out across her forehead and back.

"Wait," Ruby's voice echoed distantly, her figure distant and a shadowy silhouette at the edge of Helen's vision. "There's something more."

Despite the pull of an exciting new clue, Rosco remained at Helen's side, his hands cupping her shaking hand.

"What is it?" Rosco asked.

To Helen, his voice sounded as though he was speaking in slow motion. She allowed her heavy body to fall backwards, feeling the lumpy pressure of the mattress pushing into her back as she sank into it. She had the odd sensation of falling through a cloud.

"Are you alright?" Rosco was whispering into her ear, his face hovering above her own.

"It's a…" Ruby paused, the lilt in her voice showing her confusion, "a dagger."

Rosco's head snapped away from Helen and in the direction of the body.

"Wait, why would the victim have a knife under his pillow?" Noah mumbled, while his hand stroked his chin.

This piqued Helen's curiosity enough to push away the sickening realization that she had slept soundly a few feet from an ongoing murder. She pushed herself up onto her elbows and forced her eyes to focus on Ruby. She was holding up a dagger with an intricate hilt. It looked like something from an *Indiana Jones* prop box.

"I didn't see that last night," Helen remarked while pushing herself up onto shaky feet.

Something about the dull bronze handle and inset jewels, which she assumed were fake, did not pair well with the almost homeless appearance of Luke.

"Stolen," Ruby guessed.

"Maybe he held onto it for protection," Rosco observed.

"So, you think he knew the killer was after him?" Noah asked.

"That would explain his behavior last night. I caught him searching my bags when I came out of the bathroom. I assumed he was trying to rob me because everyone in this place seems of criminal nature, but what if he was just trying to figure out who I was?" Helen reasoned.

"What do you mean?" Ruby asked, showing her interest in Helen's theory.

"What I think I'm trying to get at is what if Luke was worried someone was looking for him, and that's why he was hiding out here. That would make him suspicious of everyone around him," Helen explained. "Suspicious enough to rifle through their stuff to see who they are, but not actually steal anything."

"It's an interesting theory, but without evidence, it's more speculation," Rosco informed her with a dubious expression.

Ruby stepped in front of Helen, almost protectively. "Noah and I have learned to pay attention to Helen's theories."

"Amateur cops would," Rosco mumbled.

Ruby looked as though she was going to sock Rosco, but Noah laid a calming hand gently on her shoulder.

"Easy," Noah whispered.

Helen's eyebrows shot up when she observed the expression exchanged between the two of them. Ruby colored slightly, a coy smile replacing the hostility she had held in place for Rosco.

"Sorry," Ruby apologized gruffly.

Helen was gob smacked. She had clearly missed a lot in the past few weeks.

"Anyway," Helen shook her head and continued. "I think that if Luke was nervous about something happening to him, then looking into his life might give us an sign of why someone was trying to kill him. And maybe this dagger is connected to that."

"Good point," Rosco agreed. "I can see why Ruby recommended you."

Helen was too focused on the dagger to hear him.

"Was it found on the left or the right?" Helen asked.

"The dagger was under the left side of his pillow," Ruby confirmed.

"Odd," Helen muttered.

"Why do you say that?" Noah asked quietly, unwilling to disturb Helen's thought process.

"Well," Helen mumbled half to herself, "if I was scared someone was going to kill me in my sleep, I would place my weapon in a place where I could grab it in the shortest amount of time."

"Like under your pillow," Rosco pointed out. "That's what he did."

Helen shook her head. "But on the wrong side. Luke was right-handed. Well, I gather that by the way he used his flask. So, logically, he would've put the dagger under the right side of his pillow so he could just reach up with his right hand, grab the knife, and surprise his attacker."

Noah nodded slowly. "I see. It makes more sense than rolling over to grab the knife from the opposite side."

Ruby walked over and stared at the knife.

"I'm sorry, Helen, but what are you getting at?" Ruby asked.

"I don't think the dagger was Luke's," Helen explained. "A dagger of this value just doesn't seem to match his persona. If it really was his, he would've sold it and bought a gun."

"Then how did the knife get here?" Rosco asked, his tone bordering on frustration.

"Simple," Helen said with a knowing smile. "The killer left it as a message."

Chapter 5
Lawyers & Apple Pie

"So, let me get this straight," Alex interrupted her, his voice firm. "A man was murdered a few feet from your bed… while you slept on peacefully…"

Helen's shoulders sank. She could hear the panic creeping into her trusted lawyer's voice.

"Helen," he sighed. "I'm worried about you."

Helen snorted. "You don't get to be worried about me. You're the one who wanted me to come on this journey."

"Helen," he crooned. "You know that when I encouraged you to hike across Eldenbourg, it's because it's what Peter wanted for you. But I can say with absolute certainty that your dead husband, my best friend, would never have wanted to put his wife in danger."

"But I'm not in danger," she reasoned.

"Really?" she could practically hear him raise his eyebrows over the phone. "A man was killed in the same room as you. And you're trying to argue with me, a lawyer -"

"The best lawyer in New York," she added.

"- that you're not in danger," he continued, ignoring the compliment. "Helen, I've told you before… I can't be responsible for something happening to you. Peter would -"

"And I've told you before," Helen cut him off, "Pete had no right to put you in charge of my safety. It's not your fault if my actions result in me getting harmed. The whole point of being single again is that I've had to learn I'm responsible for myself and I need to learn to stand on my own feet."

"I understand that," Alex said, his words saturated with exasperation, "but not when murderers are involved!"

"Alex, I need you to listen to me," Helen said, dropping her words carefully into her mobile receiver. "I'm actually helping the police with this. You, of all people, should understand how important it is to feel you're doing something meaningful with your life. I mean, you put bad people in jail, why can't I help catch them too?"

"The major difference is that my life is never in any real danger -"

"Oh, don't even go there," Helen cut him off, a smile emerging on her lips. She twirled a strand of hair while talking to him. "I remember clearly when Peter and I had to hide you and your team when you were taking down some big mafia guy. Your fight for what is right has always impressed me. Maybe that's why I've developed this passion to make a difference in the world."

"That was one time -"

"And what about when your car blew up and Peter and I spent three days believing you were dead before the police told us you were being held in witness protection until the case was over?"

Alex sighed. "Then become a lawyer. Not a police officer. You'll still be in less danger."

"You know I don't have the brains for memorizing all those laws," she laughed.

"I beg to differ. You're one of the most intelligent women I know. I believe you can do anything you put your mind to. It's something I…" he paused, and Helen discovered she was hanging on his every word. "Something I deeply… admire about you."

"Alex, I'm not in any danger. I've got three police officers I'm working with."

"I seem to recall you saying something similar last time, and that ended up in you getting kidnapped by poachers and nearly shot," Alex reminded her. "How do you know this isn't connected to the poachers you put behind bars?"

"Because of the dagger," Helen explained. "I told you, I'm convinced the killer left a dagger under the victim's pillow. I just don't know why."

"Betrayal."

"Betrayal?" Helen took a bite of her apple pie while she mulled over the concept.

"You know… Knife in the back," Alex said, in between sips of his coffee.

"You know what would help keep me safe and solve the case a lot faster?" Helen said with a coy smile.

Alex was silent for a second before he caught on. He missed nothing.

"There's no way I'm joining you in Europe," he replied, amusement evident in his voice.

"Oh, come on," Helen teased.

"I'm serious though, Helen. This sounds like a dangerous case. I can feel it in my gut. I don't want you mixed up in all this," Alex said, shifting the conversation back to its stern beginning.

Helen felt her phone being wrenched from her ear, and Ruby smirked at her as she placed Helen's cell against her own ear.

"Hi lawyer Alex," Ruby began in an official voice.

Helen clutched the table as she wondered how Alex would respond to their conversation being interrupted.

"I'm Officer Ruby Taylor. I want to assure you I will make sure Helen is safe."

Helen felt her jaw drop in surprise.

Ruby laughed. "Because Helen saved my life a few weeks back, and I admire the same things about her you do."

Helen felt her cheeks redden. She had fought with Ruby from the very first time they met. Ruby fired a wink at her across the table they were sharing, with files scattered between them.

"Alright, Alex, I'll hand the phone back to Helen so she can say bye. And Helen's right, I think you'll love Eldenbourg. We need good lawyers here."

Helen grabbed her phone back, terrified that Alex would be annoyed at the interruption, but when she pressed her ear to the speaker, he was chuckling.

"Some friends you've made. I thought the feisty officer hated you. Anyway, I'll leave you to your case, but I want you to keep me updated every day."

"I'll do that, I promise," Helen said, poking at the last mouthful of her apple pie.

"I mean it," he insisted seriously. "If I don't hear from you, I'll know something is wrong."

Helen lowered her phone. His care touched her. She could not help but notice that over the course of her adventures in Eldenbourg, which had somehow been rife with danger and mystery, Alex had grown more attached to her.

They had always been friends. She had met Alex the same day she met Peter and, while she had felt herself instantly fall for Peter, she had been equally drawn to Alex for his friendship. It had been apparent that Peter and Alex were a dual package, and she had always admired their close friendship.

Peter's death had ripped a gaping hole in both their hearts, and the only place they had found mutual comfort was in their shared grief. Alex had not left her side through more than a year of intense grieving, where Helen did not know if she could face life alone. Alex had made sure she did not have to.

"What are you thinking about?" Ruby interrupted, her face grave, as though she had picked up on the morose vibes Helen was sending off.

"I was just thinking about my history with Alex," Helen explained. "There's been something I've been meaning to ask you," Helen added quickly, so that Ruby could not press her further about Alex.

"Alright. What is it?" Ruby said, while lowering her empty pie plate and holding up a hand for the waiter.

"You used to hate me," Helen began. "Why?"

"I thought you were an interfering, know-it-all tart after - " she stopped herself when she saw Helen's distraught expression. "Well, you asked."

"Perhaps I should ask this instead. Why don't you hate me anymore?"

"Like I told your Mr. Lawyer friend. You saved my life."

"No, there's more than that."

Ruby shifted in her seat as though she was suddenly uncomfortable. She turned to the waiter who arrived.

"We'll have another two pieces of pie, but this time make it black cherry. Oh, and two more cappuccinos, please," Ruby ordered. "With cream. You were saying?"

"Okay, I'm just going to put this out there, but it felt like every time Noah talked to me, you wanted to slit my throat," Helen explained.

Ruby colored slightly. The pale blonde did not often reveal the depth of her emotions, so it surprised Helen to see the open display.

"I'm afraid you're right," Ruby admitted. "I couldn't stand you working with Noah."

"Look, Noah explained to me that the two of you used to be in a relationship, but once you were assigned as partners, he broke it off."

"He told you all that!" Ruby flushed even brighter. "You must think I'm such a cow."

"I feel like something's changed, though, and it's not just between you and me," Helen continued.

Ruby leaned in closer. "Initially, I thought Noah was completely in love with the smart, beautiful American when she walked into his station and asked for help."

"Wait, you've lost me," Helen interrupted.

"You!" Ruby moaned at her. "I'm talking about when Noah met you. You were all he could talk about, and because of my history with him, and my feelings for him, I was... I was ridiculously jealous. I'm so sorry."

Helen had not been expecting an apology. She gulped a few sips of the piping hot cappuccino that had just landed in front of her and instantly regretted it. She fanned her mouth before speaking.

"And why aren't you jealous anymore?"

"Two reasons," Ruby explained as she tucked into the golden crust of her cherry pie. "First, Noah filled me in on your husband's death. I did not know you were a widow struggling to get over the death of the love of your life. I feel so awful for judging you."

"And second?" Helen asked, desperate to understand Ruby's odd behavior.

"Second," Ruby said, hesitating. Helen could see the rise of pink in her cheeks. "Second, I realized, after poachers nearly murdered me, that Noah's feelings for me haven't changed the way I thought they had. He still wants to be in a relationship with me."

"But you work together. How will you get around that?"

"We spoke to our captain. He said as long as Noah and I split our police partnership, then we can be together romantically," Ruby explained, with excitement bubbling over. "Isn't that just amazing?"

"I think it's rather sad the pair of you won't be working together every day, but if it means you can spark your old relationship, then I'm happy for you both."

Despite her words, Helen felt something settle in the pit of her stomach, and it was not her pie. Helen could not put her finger on it. She wanted to be happy for Noah and Ruby, but part of her was also sad.

She had once believed Noah briefly interested in her, and the attention, she had to admit, was nice. Now she was back to being the lonely, sad widow, who wakes up next to dead bodies. It was depressing.

"Oh, Helen," Ruby whispered. "I had given up all hope of having genuine love."

"One thing I've learned is to never give up all hope."

"What about you then?"

"What do you mean?" Helen shoved as much pie in her mouth as she could so she would not have to answer.

This was a question Helen had avoided for the last year. At Peter's funeral, she had fled from the grandmother's and aunties wanting to nudge her in the ribs and ask if she would remarry.

"Have you given up all hope of finding another husband? I mean, you're still young, you're clever, adventurous -"

"It's..." Helen hesitated. Words evaded her brain. "I... don't really know. Pete was my everything. I can't imagine being with anyone else, but then I also find myself so alone that I do long for a companion. I'm not so sure I can let anyone new into my life when I'm still figuring out who the me without a husband is."

To her utter surprise, Ruby reached a sympathetic hand across the table and held hers.

"You've been through so much. Shall I order the peach pie next?"

"I thought I'd find you two ladies in here. Any progress on those files I gave you?" Noah asked, while slinking in next to Ruby and stealing a piece of her pie.

Helen stared at the pile of untouched files between them.

"We've kind of had other things to talk about," Ruby explained with a faint blush.

"Well, I had a chat with Boris, your landlord, and he's definitely hiding something," Noah explained.

"Did you arrest him?"

"Nothing to arrest him for. He didn't have any stolen goods on him and there was nothing else that could connect him to the crime except that you saw him there, and even then, it's your word against his," Noah explained with a sigh.

"Did you get all our samples off to the lab?" Ruby asked.

"Yes, Rosco offered to do it for me."

Ruby stiffened immediately.

"Look, I know you hate the fact that he's working our case, but there's nothing we can do about it."

"Oh really?" Ruby replied in a challenging tone. She yanked her plate of pie to herself and stared him down. "You're the superior officer here, and this is your territory. You could just tell him to leave."

Noah, his expression turning grave, leaned in closer so that only Helen and Ruby would hear what he was about to say.

"I called Rosco's station," he related in a low voice, "to find out why Rosco was snooping around our jurisdiction."

"And?" Helen and Ruby both hissed, the air between them smelling of coffee.

"And he really is here on a legitimate case," Noah continued.

"What case could be so important that it trumps our murder case?" Ruby demanded, her voice raising a few crescendos and causing more than a few heads to turn.

"Shh," Noah silenced her with a finger to her lips. Helen drew away from them, preferring not to witness their intimate moment. She focused on her pie instead, wishing she had a third and fourth slice to drown her single sorrows in.

"Jengo Prison," Noah said next.

Ruby's face paled with recognition. "No," she shook her head. "The escaped murderer?"

Noah nodded. His brown eyes flooded with concern.

"Wait," Helen waved a hand at them, "what am I missing here?"

"Didn't you hear?" Ruby asked.

"About what?" Helen snapped. "I'm not local. I don't listen to the radio or buy the paper. I look at waterfalls and gorge on your pastries."

"Yes, sorry, of course," Noah apologized. "I should've mentioned it this morning. Two days ago, Gareth the Grim escaped from a top security prison just outside Jengo."

"Jengo's close to here," Ruby continued. "The prisoner was last seen disappearing into the forest outside the prison. He could be anywhere in this area."

"And the local police don't think that this is something tourists, hiking through those same forests, should be made aware of?" Helen barked at them.

Ruby frowned. "There are posters all over town and officers put them up on the trails as soon as the station was informed. You must have missed them."

Helen scowled at the bottom of her empty coffee mug. She could feel the caffeine zing through her veins as she processed this new information.

"Does Officer Oliveira believe the murder, and the escaped convict are connected?" Helen asked.

"I'm afraid so," Noah nodded.

Helen mulled this over. There was no way she could tell Alex about this. He would have the police deliver her to the nearest airport in shackles and fly her out of the country. She shook her head and released all the pent-up air she had been holding onto. What were the chances she would encounter someone like Gareth the Grim?

"I have a picture here," Noah said, interrupting her thoughts. He pulled out his phone and showed Helen the Jengo prison photograph of their latest deserter. Helen studied the mess of brown, curly hair, and the wild forest green eyes which clashed with the orange of his overalls.

"Oh my gosh," Helen said whitening. She added a grin to the serious face of Gareth the Grim and recognized someone entirely different.

"That's just Gary."

"Who?" Ruby blurted out.

"Gary," Helen repeated, her voice scratching in her suddenly dry throat. "He's the friendly hiker I met on the trail outside of town. He said he'd lost his pack…" Helen stopped, realizing how obvious the signs were.

Gary had been wearing a shredded jacket, likely because another hiker had abandoned it. He had no pack or food, because he had just escaped from prison. And he was injured, not because he had slid down the face of a mountain, but because they had shot him.

"I stitched up his gun wound," Helen explained, cringing as she hid her face behind her hands.

"Wait, he had a bullet wound, and you still didn't think things were a little suspicious?" Noah pointed out.

Helen scowled at him. "You weren't there, okay? He was friendly and convincing. I just wanted to help."

"It's alright," Noah said, patting her hand gently. "You didn't know. I'm just glad you weren't hurt. You really are a magnet for trouble." He paused. "Do you think you could find him again?"

"Noah!" Ruby protested. "Don't you think she's been through enough?"

"Only if you're up for it, of course," Noah added with a warm smile.

"Of course, I'm up for putting a convict back behind bars!" Helen said loudly, grateful for the distraction from her loneliness.

Chapter 6
Tracking a Murderer

Helen adjusted the pack as it cut into her shoulders. She returned her gaze to the well-trodden path in front of her just in time to avoid stepping on a skittish squirrel that darted under foot.

"Jeez!" Helen exclaimed, sending a tree full of minute finches flapping away in fear.

"I can carry that for you," came the gentlemanly offer, as Rosco fell back to see what the commotion was about.

They had been hiking along the main trail for about an hour. Helen had not really known what to say, and so they had remained silent for most of the trip. Rosco seemed to have all his focus homed in on tracking the runaway Gareth the Grim.

"I'm fine, really," Helen lied.

The reality was her feet were blistering, her back ached, and she had sweated out half her body weight. They were keeping up a ridiculous pace, and Helen thought she would likely pass out before recognizing the part of the woods where she had encountered Gary.

"You don't look so good," Rosco pointed out.

Helen was suddenly self-conscious of her blazing red cheeks and clammy face. She was certain her hair stuck to her face and her eyes were dazed over from the permanent lack of oxygen. She had been trying to stifle her breathing, so Rosco would not hear how unfit she was.

"Why is he called Gareth the Grim?" Helen asked.

The question seemed to startle Rosco, and a flicker of something passed through his eyes.

"It's his prison nickname. I'm not entirely sure the sordid deeds he had to perform to be awarded such a grand title by all the other criminals, but they spoke him of with great fear."

"How do you know?" Helen continued down the list of questions she had been pondering while they walked in silence.

"My first step was to interview as many of the inmates I could. Someone at the prison had to have seen or known something, but they all protected him."

"That's rather odd. You'd think there'd be no honor among thieves," Helen remarked. "Why do you think they're protecting him?"

Rosco uttered a single word that made even the sunlit glades of green grass and wild roses seem grey.

"Fear."

"What did he do to end up in prison?" was Helen's next question.

Noah had been unwilling to share any information on the convict, and Helen's curiosity was on fire.

"He committed cold-hearted and ruthless murder," came the distant reply.

Helen could tell Rosco was in no mood to discuss Gareth. He just wanted to find him.

"What did he use? —"

"Helen," Rosco turned and interrupted her, a faint smile warming his face.

Helen nearly bumped into him. She flushed as she found her face inches from his.

"Yes?"

"Perhaps we should find something lighter to talk about. You've already been through quite the ordeal, and I feel terrible dragging you away on your holiday to help me locate someone the police let through their fingers. Let's at least make this more worth our time by getting to know each other."

"Alright," Helen agreed, though she would prefer to discuss the two cases more than anything. "Where were you born?"

"Eldenboug. Lived here my whole life. I'm from a small town on the other side of the country. You'll likely reach there in a few weeks. What about you?"

"American, as I'm sure you can tell," Helen replied with a laugh. "I grew up in the city. I love it there. So, all these trees and valleys and quaint villages have been rather inspiring to me."

He fell back, so that he was walking next to her, his shoulder brushing against hers every few steps as the path was quite cramped.

"And what do you think of our country so far?"

"It's rather crime ridden," Helen said with a laugh. "I've been involved in more police cases here than my entire life back in the states."

"How unfortunate," Rosco remarked.

"Probably because I had my husband to look after me back home. Peter kept me out of mischief."

"And why isn't Peter on this journey with you?" Rosco asked, his eyes finding Helen's.

She could have sworn she saw disappointment on his face, but she brushed it off.

"He passed away," Helen explained. At least she could say it without bursting into tears. "Just over a year ago."

Rosco stopped walking. He turned to face her, his dark eyes turning down with sadness. He enveloped her in a hug, one Helen had not expected, so she sort of just hung there, her arms limp at her sides and her face pressed into his chest. She breathed in, impressed with how good Rosco smelled after an hour in the woods. She knew she was supposed to be sad and possibly even be moved to tears, but the whole situation was unexpected. She awkwardly waited for the hug to end.

"I can't imagine what you've been through," Rosco sympathized. "I lost the love of my life, too. Though we never had a chance to get married, I've never forgotten what it took from me."

"Then you can relate," Helen replied. "Tell me, is there life after you've lost your other half?"

Rosco chuckled, though it was a distant sound considering the topic. "I'm still trying to figure that one out."

They walked on in silence, though this time Helen found it was deliberate, shared, and comfortable. They reached the fork in the road and it thrust Helen back to the day she had unknowingly cleaned up a murderer.

"Here we are," she replied.

There was a distant rumble from the sky and they both peered through the canopy of leaves above to try to decipher the weather.

"We should be fine," he assured her. "So, walk me through what happened."

Helen retraced her steps, explaining the direction Gary had come from, where she had stopped to help him, and where they had gone their separate ways. There were still some partial footprints matching her own shoes and another set of larger shoes which belonged to Gary.

"This was where I went on the path to Ochre, and he chose the opposite trail to the other village," Helen pointed down the route Gary had taken.

"It's not likely he actually made it to that village," Rosco reasoned, "not with patrols looking for him and posters everywhere. It's being broadcast on the news as well. My guess is that he's likely hiding out in the woods till he can get someone to help him disappear from society for good."

"Like a new passport and all that?" Helen asked, her mind racing through a hundred movies where that had been the main plot.

"Something like that," Rosco replied.

Another drumroll of thunder echoed through the sky, and Helen noticed the breeze had picked up as a few leaves rustled past her feet.

"We'd best get started, so have a drink or a snack, or whatever you need because we've got a long walk ahead," Rosco informed her.

Helen glanced up at the sky, which threatened to hide the sun from them in a matter of minutes. A wisp of hair blew across her face and she brushed it out, just in time to see Rosco disappear off the trail and into the woods. Helen trotted after him, unwilling to allow more than a few feet of space between them, considering there was a convict on the loose, and Luke's killer too.

"You seem to know your way around the woods," Helen observed as she struggled to keep up.

Rosco slowed down for her. "Yeah, I guess I do. I grew up playing in them with my friends."

"Sounds like a good way to grow up," Helen observed. "What was your childhood like?"

Rosco turned to her, pausing so that he could answer her.

"It was a happy one. I came from a wonderful home. My parents loved me, even though we were poor and had little. I made friends easily in school and we did everything together," he explained, his eyes flitting around the brush as though he was always on the lookout for Gareth the Grim.

"It sounds peaceful," Helen observed with a smile. "What every kid deserves."

"Oh, tragedy finds us all," he added, while continuing forward along a trail only he could sense. He would stop to study a broken twig, or a squashed mushroom, always on the lookout for Gareth's footprints. "When I was nineteen, tragedy struck our village. The girl I loved, Rosie, died, and everyone took it really hard. My friends fell away, and my parents didn't understand what I was going through. So, I had to get out of there."

"Is that why you became a police officer?" Helen asked, observing the pain written in every feature of Rosco's face.

"Yeah," he flashed a smile. "I wanted to do good in the world and prevent people from going through the same suffering I did."

"That's very noble of you," Helen said with admiration. "To be honest, when my husband died, I couldn't care what was going on in the world. I could only see my pain. I couldn't even get myself out of bed, let alone summon the energy to help other people."

Rosco had stopped again, and Helen nearly plowed into the back of him.

"And yet here you are," he said, his fingers brushing against her arm before falling away, "helping me. A complete stranger. I think you care more than you realize."

Helen smiled. "Well, I just think it gives me purpose in my life. Purpose was something I felt like I lost after Peter's death. Can I ask you a question?" Helen whispered. She gnawed on her lip while waiting for an answer.

"Sure," Rosco said, stopping again so that he could look at her.

"Do you think it's possible to love again?"

Rosco stared at the darkening sky and nodded slightly. "For so long, I didn't dare believe it possible," he replied. "You know, to feel as deeply again, or even to allow yourself to feel so strongly for another person."

"I know what you mean," Helen agreed.

"But then," he smiled, "out of the blue, you meet someone. And you catch yourself thinking, 'what if?' and it gives you, I don't know…"

"Hope?"

"Yeah," he smiled at her again. "I like that. It gives you hope that loving again is possible."

Helen nodded slowly while holding Rosco's dark gaze. She felt her own lips twitch into a smile while the pit of her stomach twisted painfully, as though berating her for being willing to hope so soon after her husband's death.

A splatter of water spat at her nose, and Helen squeaked with fright. She looked up and saw a skyful of drops pelting down in big, cold splashes.

"Oh no!" Helen cried. "What do we do now?"

Rosco shrugged. "Put on a rain jacket and keep searching. Our window is getting smaller. Every second that goes by increases our chances of never finding him."

Helen did not agree. While she saw the importance of tracking down a dangerous criminal, she did not see the need to slip off a mountain in the process. But the rain was light, and Rosco seemed confident, so she allowed him to lead her deeper into the woods.

After another hour of muddy trekking through wet leaves and dripping trees, Helen could feel the rain soak through her shoes and socks. She shivered, her mid-thigh shorts offering very little warmth. Rosco showed no signs of letting up, and Helen was struggling to see through the dark trees.

"I think we should head back," she voiced. "I'm drenched and starving, and we have found nothing. He could be anywhere."

"If we go back now, we risk the chance of losing his trail."

"Yeah, but if we carry on, we're risking our own lives," Helen reasoned.

Rosco snorted as though she was being overly dramatic and his perceived reality was that, because he was a man, he could control even the intensity of the weather and would never, no matter how extreme the circumstances, get lost.

"Just another thirty minutes and we can head back," Rosco pleaded.

Helen agreed, though the storm only seemed to draw closer with every passing minute. The crescendo of thunder seemed to split the sky above their heads and a blinding flash of lightning sent them both skittering to the nearest cave they could hide in.

"I'm sorry. We should've headed back when you suggested," Rosco informed her. "I didn't think the storm would roll in this quickly."

"It's alright," Helen said, her lips trembling and her teeth chattering. All she could think about was a steamy hot shower and a warm bowl of beef stew.

The rain was too loud for them to hold a decent conversation, so they just waited the storm out, cramped in the tiny cove. Helen tried to ignore the fact that she could feel Rosco's breath against her cheek. She wanted to shuffle in closer and cling to his warmth. As if sensing her desperation, Rosco reached an arm around Helen's shoulders and gently drew her closer to him.

"That should help," he whispered in her ear.

They stood there for some time, Helen's face buried in Rosco's chest and desperately willing away the flashes of lightning which filled the air with the buzz of electricity all around them.

Eventually, the thunder and lightning gradually retreated, as though exhausted from the spectacular display of power. The pelting rain eased up to a gentle drizzle and the surrounding air lightened as the sun fought through the heavy clouds.

It was a slippery and uncomfortable walk back to the main trail. Helen lost her footing several times and cut her knee on a sharp rock. The body parts which were not soaked were scratched and scraped, or covered in mud. To her relief, once they reached the road, Rosco pointed to a quad he had arranged to fetch them.

He took the driver's seat and urged her to hold tight before he sped off along the muddy track, flicking mud up behind them and skidding dangerously close to the edge of the trail. She gripped her arms tight around his torso, leaning her cheek on his damp back and thinking about how any clues of Gareth the Grim would have been lost in the downpour which washed the forest clean of any human trace.

Rosco finally stopped the quad outside Boris's dreadful inn.

"I'll fetch you in thirty minutes?" he cast over his shoulder while Helen slowly forced icy joints to move again as she climbed off the back.

"Sorry?"

"For dinner. It's the least I can do after everything I put you through today," Rosco explained.

At the mention of a hot meal, Helen's stomach betrayed her with a loud and embarrassing grumble.

"I'll be ready in twenty."

Helen walked towards the front door, but suddenly paused. She turned back to see if Rosco was still watching her, but he was gone. The hairs on her neck prickled, and again she felt as though she was being watched. She scanned her surroundings and saw the faintest flicker of something dark, but then it was gone.

Probably Agatha.

Probably.

Chapter 7
Midnight Revenge

Helen threw herself over onto her other shoulder, trying to ignore the uncomfortable lumps that poked into her hips and ribs. She pulled out her phone and checked the time. It was one in the morning. She sighed heavily; her annoyance directed solely at Boris.

Helen had enjoyed the most delightful dinner with Rosco. They had chatted easily for hours about their backgrounds and hopes for the future. Helen was thoroughly interested in how he had become a police officer, whereas Rosco was more interested in life in America.

She had returned home with her cheeks glowing from some rather vintage port and the most delicious leg of lamb she had ever gorged on, not to mention the thrill of enjoying the company of a rather handsome man.

Boris had rapidly destroyed her good mood. Upon her arrival, she had found that not only had all her luggage disappeared, but the police had taped the entire bunkroom off. Helen stormed up to the reception and was immediately accosted by Agatha, who wove her way between Helen's legs, rattling off a husky, yet delighted, purr.

"I can't believe my cat actually likes someone," Boris observed dryly.

"We shared a bed," Helen explained gruffly. "Look, I don't want to stay here anymore than you don't want me here, but I have no other choice. All the other places are full."

"I'm not kicking you out," Boris said in a snively voice. "On the contrary, I've given you an upgrade."

"What are you talking about?"

"The police demanded I close the crime scene, so I've had to move you to a private room."

It rather surprised Helen at the pleasant turn of events. She had not been looking forward to spending the night alone in the same space Luke had been murdered in. The air in the bunkroom felt tainted with hatred.

"Why thank you, Boris." Helen offered him a prim smile and turned to leave.

"However," Boris paused so that Helen would turn back to face him.

"Yes," Helen groaned.

"A private room incurs a greater expense. So, you'll have to cover the difference this evening before I can give you the key to your room."

"Are you insane?" Helen asked, her voice raising.

Agatha hissed at Helen, and her oily fur stood on end.

"I've already paid double for several nights in the bunkroom," Helen explained.

"It's not enough. Take it or leave it. I'm sure you could find somewhere else to stay… oh wait," he delivered a sinister smile, which gave her the creeps in the almost green light emitted by a single candle.

"Fine," Helen grumbled. "What do I owe you?"

She nearly fainted at the exorbitant price, but not having much of a choice, Helen slapped the notes down on the counter.

"You're a wicked man, you know that?" Helen barked at him. "Now, where's the key?"

"For my more trusted guests, I don't require a key deposit, but unfortunately, your hostility has left me no choice."

Helen was ready to leap over the counter between them and throttle him with her bare hands. He must have seen the malevolent look in her eye, because he quickly slid the heavy key across the counter.

"I'll make an exception this time," he informed her before turning away. "You'll find your bags are already there."

Helen snatched the key and stomped out of the reception area. Her skin pricked with cold as the warmth of the fire in the reception room faded from memory.

She stalked up the narrow set of stairs and found the door with her name pinned to it. The key was ancient, and it took several tries before she unlocked the door and burst into the dusty quarters.

That had been several hours before. Helen was still seething at having paid more for a set of dusty sheets, moldy curtains, and a leaky basin which offered coppery colored water to brush her teeth in.

After another uncomfortable turn, which allowed an icy draft through the broken paneling to grip round her toes and creep up her legs, Helen had had enough. She cast the holey blanket aside, stormed past Agatha, and wedged her feet into her bunny shaped slippers. Helen then crept out of her room and back towards reception.

Boris was nowhere in sight, and Helen had made sure she had locked Agatha in her room so that the pesky cat could not sound the alarm when she went poking around Boris's office. She snuck into his office, which was oddly unlocked, and stifled a gasp when she spotted all the luxury Boris kept for himself.

Her flashlight scanned over a state-of-the-art coffee machine, a fridge filled with chocolate tarts, unbaked croissants, and what looked like a colorful array of macaroons.

"Can you believe this guy?" she mumbled to herself.

Although considering the amount of cash he had made off her, it was not surprising at all when she walked across the sheep skin rug, seated herself in the most comfortable chair she had ever fallen into and pulled open a drawer overflowing with neat bundles of cash. She picked up his jewel encrusted pen to calculate the total amount of money Boris had stolen from her.

While looking for paper, she came across something else which chilled her to the bone. It was a familiar looking flask. Helen knew immediately that it had been the flask Luke had drunk from the night before he was murdered. This confirmed that Boris had been stealing from him that morning.

She flicked on the crystal desk lamp and noticed a brown glass bottle sealed in a Ziplock bag. There was still liquid inside. Helen pulled the bag open and withdrew the bottle, careful to only touch it with Kleenex, in case it was what she thought it was.

There was no label, but a single sniff confirmed her suspicions.

Chloroform.

Helen's heart was pulsing as she reached for her phone and composed a text at lightning speed. Noah had said there was not enough evidence to arrest Boris, but she was fairly sure that procuring the bottle of chloroform used to drug Luke before killing him would be sufficient.

"What are you doing?" a voice attacked in the dark.

Helen was trying to duck under the desk when the lights flicked on and Boris, wearing crimson satin pajamas, was standing with his arms folded across his hairy chest while he stared at her.

"I knew something was wrong when I heard Agatha shrieking like she was being murdered in your room."

"Boris," Helen began, her voice quavering. "I know what you did."

"You do?"

"And I'm going to do something about it!" Helen said loudly, trying to suppress the fear she felt with increased volume.

"It was only a few photographs, and you were still fully clothed," Boris spluttered.

"Wait, what?" Helen squeaked as she realized what he was saying. "I'm talking about murder!"

"Murder?" Boris stammered. "Like I said to Officer Wolff, I'm no murderer."

"I saw you over Luke's body," Helen accused.

"I was making sure he had enough blankets," Boris replied defensively.

"I found the chloroform you used to drug him!" Helen practically shouted.

"Chloroform?" Boris repeated, his heavy eyebrows knitting in the middle. "That stuff works? I thought that was just in the movies."

"Boris!" She pointed at the bottle on his desk. "Why do you have this?"

"That's not mine," he said with a shake of his head. "I would leave nothing like that lying around."

Helen scowled at him. She had thought it rather odd that every single item in Boris's office seemed to have its proper place, whereas the chloroform was placed randomly on the desk.

"It's a little hard to believe you when you seem dishonest to the core," Helen thrust the accusation at him. "You ripped me off several times. In fact, you rip off everyone who stays here, pretending that you don't know any better, whereas you're actually using all your money to pamper yourself instead of looking after your guests properly. Besides, I found you standing over a dead body stealing from him!"

Helen paused. Boris had not been protesting her accusations as she had expected. Instead, the tall, big-framed man had dropped his head into his hands and was quietly sobbing.

"Oh jeez," Helen sighed. "You're crying?"

He shook his head and the runnels of tears down his cheeks indicated he had not been faking the wave of emotion that had overtaken him.

"Boris," Helen said with a sigh. "I simply don't understand you."

"I'm… I'm…" he blubbered, wiping his tears on his silk sleeve. "I'm not a murderer!"

"The facts state otherwise," Helen replied harshly.

"I could kill no one! Why do you think this place is infested with rats? I can't bring myself to poison them all, so I leave Agatha to kill as many as she can while I turn a blind eye."

"Maybe if you fed Agatha less steak, she would be more inclined to kill the pests," Helen explained. "But seriously, Boris, you're in real trouble. This evidence is incriminating. You're going to have to come up with something a little more convincing."

Boris looked up at her and he breathed deeply, as though trying to compose himself.

"Alright," he agreed, "I'll tell you the truth. I have a slight problem with…" he paused, his wide eyes imploring her to silence him.

Helen raised an eyebrow. "Go on."

He scowled at her. "I have a problem with pretty things, okay? It's no big deal, and it's perfectly under control, but now and then," his eyes settled on the shiny hip flask Luke had used, "I see something I fancy, and," his fingers started wriggling in the air as though electrified, "I just can't help but touch. And then after I touch, I want it to be mine and then I don't know what happens after that."

"I can tell you what happens," Helen replied dryly. "It's called stealing. Now be honest, did you steal anything from me?"

She watched as Boris's puffy face crumpled into one of pitiful regret.

"I can't help it!" he wailed into the air as though tortured by his sins.

"What did you take?" Helen demanded, her arms wrapping protectively around her while she mentally worked through the contents of her pack.

"Just most of your money and this ring," Boris admitted. He held up his pinky, and Helen recognized her wedding ring.

"You stole my wedding ring!" she erupted.

Agatha scampered under an armchair in fright. It was the first time Helen had ever seen the cat afraid.

"If it was important to you, I figured you'd be wearing it," Boris pointed out with a pathetic simper.

"I'm not wearing it because I'm terrified I'll lose it while hunting down convicts through the woods, so I put it there for safe keeping," Helen explained, ignoring the guilt that gnawed at her.

"I just thought you didn't want that nice Officer Rosco to know you are married," Boris said with a sly wiggle of his eyebrows.

Helen narrowed her gaze on the middle-aged man in pajamas even more ridiculous than her own. She had visions of herself launching across his expensive cherry wood desk and yanking her ring off his hand with her teeth.

"I'll have you know," she growled like a feral cat, "that my husband is dead, and that ring is my daily reminder of the beauty we once shared. Give," she took a step around the desk, "it," she took another calculated step, "back!" she roared, ready to launch at him with all the strength she possessed.

"Alright!" Boris shrieked like a sixteen-year-old girl. "Take it!"

He was trying to pry it from his pinky when Helen grabbed his hand with hers.

"Pull it off!" she squealed in frustration. "Either you pull it off, or I'll cut it off!"

Boris withdrew his hand to his chest and he cowered away from her.

"You're a monster!" he whined.

"At least I don't rob dead bodies!" Helen hissed.

"Do you think we should interrupt them or see how the fight plays out?" Noah said dryly to Rosco, who was watching from the entrance to the office.

"I reckon Boris could get pretty hurt," Rosco reasoned, a smile creeping across his lips. "Best we get involved."

"I'm warning you, Boris, I'm going to feed Agatha to the fishes!" Helen shouted while holding Boris' cat up to the ceiling fan, which was off but it created the right mental picture.

"Alright!" Boris shouted. "Here," he shoved the ring in her hand. "Now leave me alone, you wretched woman!"

"I think we'll take it from here," Noah announced loudly so that Helen could hear him.

"Noah," Helen gasped. "How long have you been here?"

"Long enough to know you're not afraid to murder a cat to get your jewelry back," Rosco pointed out while stifling a laugh.

"This is outrageous," Boris complained. "Arrest this woman at once. I'll not be insulted like this in my home."

"I'm afraid," Noah said with a tired sigh as he stepped up to Boris, "that you're the one under arrest."

"On what grounds?"

"Because you have chloroform in your office when it was a drug used on Luke McCray," Rosco stated while moving forward with a set of handcuffs.

"Like I told the interfering little lady," Boris stated firmly, "that bottle is not mine. I've never seen it before in my life!"

"Though Boris is a bit of a weirdo," Helen interrupted, while quietly trying to force her wedding ring back on her ring finger. She had certainly gained more than a few pounds while on holiday. "I don't see how Boris has a motive to kill Luke. Surely, he needs cause to be a suspect."

"We heard it out of his own mouth," Rosco said as he slapped a cuff on Boris's one hand. "Boris likes pretty things. It's no surprise that he would kill for those pretty things."

"Preposterous!" Boris objected.

"Noah..." Helen said his name hoping he could help.

"I'm sorry, Helen, but we need to take Boris down to the local station. Try to get some sleep and we can talk in the morning."

Chapter 8
Visiting the Prisoner

Helen got little sleep after the episode in Boris's office. She could not stop working through all the clues she had uncovered. There was the odd knife. If Boris liked pretty things, then why would he leave the most valuable object on Luke, unless he had not seen the knife?

Then there was his bizarre office filled with spectacular things, each in a specific place so that he could admire their beauty. Why would he leave a smudgy bottle of chloroform lying on his desk, especially if he really had used it to commit a murder?

Helen started feeling more and more guilty since she was the one who had summoned Noah to Boris's office. She even allowed Agatha to creep onto the corner of her bed, where she wrapped the straggly cat in a bit of blanket.

"You know I'd never hurt you," Helen whispered to the forlorn cat in the grey light of early morning. "It was just a threat."

The cat stretched and turned its head so that it could not see Helen, which added to her guilt even more.

Once the sun was fully up, Helen grabbed breakfast for two in the village square and then she hurried over to the police station. When Rosco saw her, a wide smile spread across his face and his eyes flitted down to the bacon and cheese croissant in her hand.

"You shouldn't have," he said with a wink.

Helen blushed awkwardly. "I'm afraid I didn't. This is for Boris."

"The alleged murderer?" Rosco barked in shock.

"I'm not so sure he is a murderer," Helen confided in him.

"The results from the lab confirm that the substance found on Luke is the same as the chloroform found in Boris's office," Rosco stated matter-of-factly, before marching off.

Helen waited till he was out of sight before sneaking off to the holding room she knew was located somewhere at the back of the station. They built all the stations in Eldenbourg in a similar design. She weaved in between unobservant officers and found herself in front of Boris's human cage.

"Good morning," she greeted him.

He at least had a robe over his pajamas. Not that the police had ever afforded her that luxury.

"I brought you breakfast," she said, thrusting the croissant and still hot cappuccino through the bars.

"Is it poisoned?" he practically spat at her.

"Of course not," Helen scolded him. "I fed Agatha this morning. I was right, you feed her steak."

His glower softened at the mention of his darling cat, and he accepted the extended food.

"Thank you, though I don't quite understand why you're doing all of this when you're the one who tried to get me arrested," he said with a sullen bite of his croissant.

"I know," Helen said, taking a seat next to him and staring at him through the bars. "I just saw that bottle and jumped to conclusions. Of course, now I realize it could easily have been planted there. Has anyone other than me been near your office?"

Boris thought for a moment. "I don't see how. I always keep it locked."

"Always?" Helen asked, chewing on a fingernail.

"Always."

"It was unlocked when I went to your office," Helen recalled.

"Not possible," Boris denied. "I have the key around my neck."

"Boris, I'm serious. The door was unlocked."

"Do you think…" he paused, his eyes wide with terror, "someone was trying to rob *me*? I mean, I know I deserve it, but the prospect is terrifying."

"No, Boris, I think someone is trying to frame you," Helen explained.

"Who would do such a thing?"

"The actual murderer. Look, I'm going to get you out of here, but I need to find more clues first."

"What about that convict on the loose?" Boris pointed out. "Why am I locked up, and a known murderer is running around out there? You know, I swear I saw him lurking around my cottage last night. I bet it was him."

"Alright, calm down," Helen soothed him. "I'll be back when I can."

Helen darted out of the holding room and went in search of Noah, but he was not in yet. Nor was Ruby. She wondered if they would come in together and again felt the unwanted pang of jealously ripple through her stomach. She knocked on Rosco's door, but there was no response, so she let herself in.

If she was perfectly honest, she had not planned to snoop through his things, but since there was a pile of files on his desk and no Rosco in sight, Helen could not resist taking a peek. She flipped through a few of the old files and the first thing she spotted was a knife. At first, she thought it was a photograph of the knife they found in Luke's bed, but upon closer inspection, she realized it was different.

The hilt was gold, and the jewels looked real. One major difference was that the dagger in the photograph was encrusted with dried blood to the hilt, whereas the knife in Luke's bed had been clean. She flipped the file closed to read the name on the front cover and discovered Gareth Grey written across the front. Helen's mouth was suddenly dry, and she shook her head.

"It's not possible," she whispered.

But the facts were right in front of her. It could not be coincidence that the week Gareth the Grim escaped from prison was the same week a man was murdered with a replica of the first murder weapon. She raced through the files, trying to absorb as much information as she could, until she stumbled across another photograph that she recognized.

"Luke," she said out loud, her finger stroking the pale face of a much younger Luke McCray. He looked as though he was barely out of school.

"What are you doing?"

Helen jumped so hard she rammed her back into the bookshelf behind her.

"Rosco," the name caught in her throat. "I'm sorry. This is none of my business."

He was scowling at her. A look she was relatively used to in the police department. One would think officers would appreciate all the help they could get, but on the contrary, it always appeared they despised her meddling.

"Wait," he latched a hand onto her forearm. "I'm not angry. Tell me what you think."

"I don't think Boris is your murderer," Helen began.

"Based on?"

"Because I think he was framed," Helen continued.

"By?"

"Gareth the Grim."

"And your proof?" Rosco asked, his features revealing nothing about how he felt about the information.

"The knife."

"I see," Rosco nodded. "It could be a copycat."

Helen shook her head. "Luke was targeted."

"Why?"

"Because he was a witness responsible for putting Gareth behind bars. He witnessed the murder," Helen explained. "And I think that's why Gareth broke out of jail and killed him. It's all revenge for the betrayal he believes Luke is responsible for."

"Is this true?" Noah's voice sounded behind Rosco.

Rosco turned around and sighed.

"I only just discovered it myself," Rosco explained. "Come in."

Ruby and Noah filed into the cramped office Rosco had temporarily claimed as his own. He flicked on the coffee machine and pulled four mugs out of a cupboard.

"After we booked Boris last night, I couldn't shake the feeling that none of this felt right. Boris might be crazy, but he's been stealing from guests for decades without getting caught, so it's not likely he'd leave the murder weapon lying on his desk," Rosco pointed out.

"Go on," Noah urged, after pouring himself a cup of coffee.

"I came back here and scoured through all the old case files from the Grey murder. And I found believable connections."

"Like the knife," Helen agreed. "It has to be Gareth."

"Were there other witnesses in the case?" Ruby asked. "If so, they could be Gareth's next target. What if he's planning on eliminating everyone who put him behind bars?"

Helen felt a tremor work its way down her spine.

"Then there's something you should all know," Rosco said with a shadow passing over his face. As if to keep them in suspense, he walked over to the coffee machine and poured Helen a cup and then himself. "There was a second witness to Gareth's murder."

"Okay, so who was it?" Ruby blurted, with a frustrated flick of her hair over her shoulder.

"Me."

Helen clutched her hand to her mouth in shock. "You! Why didn't you say anything?"

"That explains your crazy emotional attachment to this case," Ruby retorted, and her cheeks flushed with anger. "Do your supervisors even know?"

"That's why I was put on this case. I know Gary. We were friends our whole lives until…"

He drifted off, his face fading to an unhealthy shade of grey.

"I think it's best you tell us the complete story," Noah insisted.

"That's why I called you in here. Look, I didn't know Luke was in town until we found the dead body."

"So why waste time with arresting Boris?" Helen interrupted.

"Because that's what Gareth wanted us to do. And if he's following the news, or rumors from the station, he would believe that we'd fallen for his set up," Rosco explained.

"You put us all in danger by withholding this information," Ruby fired at him. "How dare you!"

"Do you want the truth or not?"

Ruby did not reply. She glared at Noah as though it was also somehow his fault for not picking up on Rosco's deception.

"That's not all. Luke, Gary, and I were friends through school. There was a fourth member of our group, and her name was Rosemary, though she joined later," Rosco explained, his eyes distant as though he could see the characters right in front of him. "Rose and I fell in love almost instantly and I think Gary was always jealous of that."

"Things were fine until we graduated. Gary and I wanted to go to college and make something of ourselves. Luke was never really sure what he wanted to do. He kind of followed us around and was always on the fence. I thought he was most likely to end up the criminal, not Gareth."

"So what happened?"

"Gareth's parents died in an accident. It brought out a really dark side in him. He needed money and somewhere to stay. Rose was incredibly wealthy and generous, and she always had a soft spot for Gary, so she told him he could stay with us. Things were okay, but then we noticed small things were missing. A pair of diamond earrings. A painting from the hallway."

"Gary?" Helen guessed.

Rosco nodded, his eyes dark and his blonde hair a mess over his brow. Heavy rings encircled his eyes, and it was clear he had not slept in a long time.

"I tried to talk to him. It didn't go down well. We got into a big fight. I searched his bag and found the dagger in the photos. It belonged to Rose's parents and was some ancient artifact or other. He knew it would fetch a high price, so he took it from her, without a care in the world for the friends who had done everything they could to help him."

The air in the room was static with anticipation. Even Ruby remained silent. Helen simply gripped her coffee mug, ignoring the pain as the porcelain burnt into her hand.

"It happened so fast. Rose came out of nowhere and tried to wrestle for the knife. Gary just lost it. I don't even think he knew what he was doing until the knife disappeared into her chest for the third time. I must have blacked out at some point because when I came around, all I remember is Luke screaming, Rosie bleeding out on the rug, and Gary was gone."

Helen slipped her arm around Rosco's shoulder, but she felt as though she was holding a stone statue in her arms. Reliving the experience had drained him of any warmth and love.

"What did you do after that?" Ruby asked. Even her petulant features were softened with empathy.

"Luke wanted to run, but..." Rosco's hands trembled, and he looked as though he was fighting back tears. "I convinced him to stay and testify. If it weren't for me, Luke would still be alive."

He hid his face behind a hand as he struggled to regain control of his emotions.

"No," Helen said gently, placing a hand on his forearm. "If it weren't for Gary, Luke would still be alive. You can't carry guilt like this. You're not the one who killed them."

"She's right," Noah agreed. "You need to put thoughts like that out of your mind. They're only going to hinder you in catching Gareth."

"I think you need to be pulled from this case," Ruby stated firmly. "It's obvious your life is in danger, and we want no more casualties. We will track him down for you."

Rosco shook his head and shrugged back his shoulders. "I can't let you do that. This is something I need. I have to catch him. It's the only thing I live for. My fight for justice."

"Well, we're fighting the same fight, buddy," Noah said with a hearty slap on Rosco's back. "We're here to help."

"So, what's the plan, then?" Ruby asked, still uneasy about having to work with Rosco.

"We lay a trap for him," Rosco explained.

"And what are we going to use to draw him in?" Noah asked with a frown.

Helen shook her head. She feared that she already knew the answer.

"Me," Rosco said with a wild grin.

Chapter 9
Gareth the Grim

Helen practically danced down the path to Boris's front door. She had enjoyed dinner with Rosco again. She had spent a considerable amount of time convincing herself that it was not a date and that she was simply trying to console a friend after a hard day.

Her phone buzzed in her pocket and she pulled it out.

"Oh, hey, Alex," she said with a smile spreading across her face. "I just had the most glorious evening."

"Does that mean the murder case is solved?" came the concerned reply.

"Not yet."

"Then it's all the wine," Alex said with a chuckle.

"Alex," Helen stopped to throw her head back and study the stars which beamed down on her, "I think I've met someone."

There was a long pause on the other end of the line.

"He's just so brave and courageous and he's been through the same trauma of losing the love of his life as I have," Helen rattled on, feeling the gush of emotion well up in her. "Would it be so wrong to think we could be each other's second options?"

"I…" Alex hesitated. She could hear him take a deep breath on the other end of the line. *"I didn't realize you were ready to move on."*

Helen felt a flood of guilt. "Oh, no, I'm not. I still cry for Pete every night. But if he's willing to just be my friend for a few years, I'm sure I'll grow a love for him."

"Helen."

He was serious. She hated it when he used her name like that.

"Yes, Alex," she said with an eye-roll.

"I just think it's a little too soon. You hardly know this guy, and you're in the middle of a murder investigation."

Helen started giggling. "I forgot to tell you there's an escaped jail convict on the loose, too. We think he may be the killer."

There was a stunned silence on the other end of the line.

"Helen, I want you to listen -"

"Oh, Alex," she sighed. "The stars are just so beautiful tonight. I wish you were here with me. We could dance together, under the moonlight. Remember how we always danced together because Peter had two left feet?"

"I remember," he said warmly. *"I've always loved dancing with you."*

Helen suddenly grew sorrowful. The memories of her husband and time with his best friend were too much.

"I miss you," she croaked into the phone. "I'm going to say good night."

And with that, Helen hung up, shoved her phone in her bag, which took far longer than it should have, and turned to go into the cottage, but found the entrance blocked.

"You," she said, her hazy vision focusing long enough for her to recognize the mess of wild hair and the green eyes that flashed even in the moonlight.

She tried to turn and run, but a powerful hand covered in a filthy bandage restrained her. She tried to scream, but a second hand wrapped over her mouth.

"Just be quiet and I won't hurt you," came the hiss of a whisper hot against her ear.

Helen felt herself being dragged backward. The wine had numbed her senses and made her careless. The lights of the cottage disappeared behind thick bushes and tree branches as Gareth the Grim carried her into the depths of the forest. Then even the stars and moon disappeared as Gareth pulled her into a musty cave.

She readied herself for the chloroform. The knife. Or whatever else Gary had intended to do to her. To her surprise, he lowered her gently to a mattress, her feet slipping against the slick material of a sleeping bag. Next, he switched on a small lantern which cast a warm glow around the cold cavern.

"What do you want with me?" Helen demanded, trying to make her shaky voice sound as fierce as possible.

"I just want to talk," he said while binding her hands and feet. "These are just so you don't whack me over the head and run away."

"What would I have to say to a killer?" Helen hissed in her face, willing her words to cause as much pain as possible.

Gary cupped his warm hand over her bound ones and looked her square in the eyes, the flickering lantern giving the impression that his eyes were twinkling at her.

"Come on," he whispered. "Look into my eyes. There's no killer in here."

Helen scoffed, turning her gaze away from him. "I read the files. I saw the photos of that poor girl. And I heard the truth from an eyewitness. You're a murderer!"

Gareth stopped her with a hand to the mouth.

"Don't say that," he pleaded, more than commanded. "Is this the girl in the photos?" he asked, holding up a damaged photograph that looked as though it had been folded a hundred times over.

Helen squinted and nodded.

"This," Gareth said with a smile as he brought the photo up to his lips and kissed it, "is my Rosemary."

"You mean Rosco's Rosie."

Gareth's eyebrows spiked, and he beheld her for a moment. "Still telling that story, is he?"

Gareth focused on the photograph again and took a second to unfold the second half. Helen drew it close to her nose and still could not believe what she was seeing. A man was kissing Rosemary's cheek, which accounted for the gleeful smile on her face.

"But that's you," Helen realized. "Not Rosco. I don't understand."

"Will you let me tell you a truth that no one has cared to listen to for the last decade?" Gary asked, his eyes almost mad with desperation.

Helen nodded. She felt compelled to.

"Throughout school, it was me, Rosco, and Luke. We were like a pack of wild dogs, free to roam the woods and do as we pleased. I grew up poor, but I had two amazing parents who loved me. Anyway, it was just the three of us until Rosie moved into our high school. She was the new kid, so everyone kind of ignored her and teased her. But I thought she was the prettiest girl alive, so I made friends with her. It wasn't long after that before I was completely in love."

Helen opened her mouth to speak, but Gary held up his hand for her to stay silent.

"Rosie joined our group, and I noticed Rosco was pretty keen on her, too. Well, he found out she was some diplomat's daughter and was actually crazy rich. Anyway, to my surprise, Rosie chose poor, completely ungifted me. We graduated, and we'd all went our separate ways. Luke was going to stay in town. Rosco was going to college. And I wanted to stick with Rosie. We were going to travel the world together."

Helen studied Gary's face, which seemed to radiate warmth as he spoke with fondness about the mysterious Rosie who seemed to be the love of two men's lives.

"Rose and I moved in together. It was bliss. But then Rosco's parents died in a flood. His entire house collapsed, and he needed somewhere to stay, so we offered him a room at our place. I thought it was great, but Rosie wasn't that comfortable with it. She complained about how Rosco looked at her. Anyway, we put up with it, but things got worse."

"What do you mean?" Helen could not help but ask.

"Rosco. It's like he was jealous. No matter what I had, even if it was a poor kid's life working on a farm, he wanted it. When I had Rosie, he wanted no other girl but her."

"Rosco said he grew up poor on a farm. He said Rosie was in love with him and that it was your parents who died in an accident."

Gary shook his head. "One day, I came home from work and Rosie and Rosco were in an argument. Luke was trying to calm them down, but it wasn't working. Rosco was begging Rosie to choose him and run away with him. She refused, and then things turned ugly.

I tried to intervene, but Rosco grabbed a knife from the display. He went for me first," he explained, pulling down the neckline of his t-shirt and revealing an ugly scar. "But then Rosie pushed herself between us and she took the next stab wound. I think it was only on the third stab that Rosco realized it wasn't me."

"No," Helen gasped, her stomach sick. "This doesn't make sense. If Rosco was the actual killer, why would Luke testify otherwise?"

"Rosco's money eventually came through from his parents' will and, from what I can figure, he either threatened Luke or offered him considerable money to tell his version of things."

"Gary," Helen shook her head. "I want to believe you, but to be honest, you're the escaped convict who kidnapped me. Rosco has been nothing but good to me."

"I didn't mean to kidnap you," he explained. "I've been watching you, looking for an opportunity to talk, but you're always surrounded by cops."

"I can't believe you just in words," Helen said. "Rosco has actual evidence."

"Then find the proof."

"What?"

"Find the proof I need. I escaped from jail so I could prove my innocence and go home to my parents, a free man. Luke was going to testify to the truth, and then he was murdered. Now I'm desperate, out of options. I really need your help to find proof."

"I can't promise to find proof," Helen reasoned. "But I will do my best to uncover the truth. Whatever that may be."

Gary raised her bound hands to his lips, and he kissed them gently. "Thank you," he whispered, his eyes filling with grateful tears.

Helen felt as though the weight of the world had suddenly shifted onto her shoulders. How was she to prove this man's innocence when she was not entirely certain he really was innocent?

"One more thing," he said, interrupting her thought process. "Could you clean my wound up again before you go?"

Chapter 10
The Trap

A glance at her phone revealed several missed calls from Alex. She swiped them away and pulled up Ruby's number.

"I need a favor," she said as soon as Ruby picked up.

Twenty minutes later, Helen handed Ruby a tall coffee and a donut.

"A little stereotypical, don't you think?" Ruby scoffed, though Helen noticed she snatched at the donut and did not let it go.

Ruby slipped into the station. "Follow me."

"Is he there?" Helen hissed into Ruby's ear.

Ruby shook her head. "All clear."

Ruby and Helen quickly scuttled along the passage and into Rosco's office. The advantage of being a station in a small town was that the one or two officers on night duty were fast asleep or on their hundredth episode of *Friends*.

"See if you can log in to his computer," Helen instructed.

Ruby hesitated, her fingers hovering over the keyboard. "I need to ask you something. Why did you call me? Why not Noah?"

"Because you seemed to have doubts about Rosco from the beginning. I thought you might be most likely to believe me," Helen explained.

Ruby nodded. "Fair enough. But do you really think Rosco is the actual killer? It just seems so farfetched. I know I have my issues with the guy, but to hide a murder all these years while your former best friend rots in jail seems a little extreme. He's a cop for crying out loud.

"I don't know what to believe," Helen said while paging through Rosco's files on the case. She stumbled across his own testimony and scanned through it. It was as though Rosco and Gareth were both claiming the same story as their own. Though she knew someone was secretly playing the role of murderer.

"It makes me sick to think there could be criminals among us posing as officers of the law," Ruby continued, clearly shaken by Gareth's claims. "Let's see what we can find."

"As far as I can tell, there has to be some kind of connection between Luke and Rosco. Why was Luke here? And if Gareth didn't kill him, then it had to have been Rosco."

"Maybe Rosco thought Luke was going to betray him," Ruby reasoned. "Right, I'm logged in. I'll start looking around."

"Start with his email. Not his work one, obviously."

Ruby nodded, her fingers tapping away vigorously as she glared at the screen. Helen peered over her shoulder, eager to find anything to exonerate a man she had grown quite fond of.

"You reek of wine," Ruby pointed out.

"Sorry," Helen apologized. "I was out on a date with Rosco, actually."

Ruby froze. "Hold up. You're asking me to investigate the man you've been silently falling for?"

"I know," Helen whined. "It's so messed up. My heart is in turmoil."

"Have you told your lawyer friend Alex about all this?"

"I haven't called him back. But I may have mentioned my crush on Rosco in my semi-inebriated state earlier," Helen explained with a flush of her cheeks.

"Alex couldn't have been too impressed. I'm pretty sure he's keen on you," Ruby stated confidently. "Anyway, I've hacked Rosco's email."

Helen was pacing behind Ruby. "Wait, why would you say he's keen on me?"

"Helen, shut up a second," Ruby urged, waving a hand at Helen. "I've found something."

Helen poked her head over Ruby's shoulder and read the string of emails Ruby was rapidly scrolling through.

"Oh, this is good. Well done, Ruby. I think it's time we update Noah."

***

"Why exactly did we have to move the trap up?" Rosco asked, his voice groggy. "And where are the others?"

"It's less suspicious this way," Helen replied. "Gareth won't be expecting you at three in the morning. The others are on their way."

"And how do you know Gareth will be here?" Rosco whispered.

"I didn't tell you this because I wasn't sure. But the last couple of weeks, I've been feeling like someone is following me. You know, a shadow moving, a stick cracking."

"He's probably tracking you to get close to me," Rosco explained. He pulled his gun from his pocket and loaded it. "I'll stay hidden. Let's see if he approaches."

"It's so sad to think that years ago, you were all close friends. I was thinking more about the stories you told me from your childhood. You know, about Rosie and the others."

Rosco shoved his gun back in his holster and sat down next to her. "I told you, I'm finally ready to move on from Rosie," he said, placing a hand on hers. "I just hope there's a part of you that's ready to move on, too."

"The thing is," Helen said, carefully slipping her hand away. "I heard a similar story about Rosie from someone else."

Rosco stared at her while trying to make sense of her words.

"Someone else claims Rosie was the love of their life and that she was cruelly taken from him," Helen continued, her eyes glued to Rosco's face as it turned deathly pale.

"What are you talking about?" Rosco demanded, his eyes cold and lifeless.

"She's talking about me," Gareth said, stepping silently into view like a dark shadow. "The stories you've been claiming as your own are mine."

Rosco leapt forward, his hand reaching immediately for his holster, but his gun was no longer there. He looked frantically around and found Helen smiling at him.

"You!" He glared at her.

"Not so fast, Rosco, old buddy. It's time you look me in the eye and tell the truth," Gareth insisted. "I've paid for your murder long enough."

"You're insane!" Rosco growled at him, his dark eyes wild with panic. "You're the convict. You killed Rosie. And you killed Luke to get revenge for testifying against you."

"On the contrary," Helen replied, "we found your deleted email thread between you and Luke. Luke had contacted you, Rosco. Shortly after Gareth had written to Luke from prison, offering him a high price to tell the truth and free Gareth, Luke emailed you asking for a higher price. He really was a rat, ready to sell his version of the truth to the highest bidder."

This was news to Gareth. He had been counting on Luke's promised testimony. He shook his head and sighed.

"Luke had betrayed me once," Gareth said sadly, "so I shouldn't be all that surprised that he will do it again for a higher paycheck from Rosco."

"That's why there was a dagger under the pillow," Helen explained to Rosco. "You were using it to frame Gareth, of course, but it was also a message to anyone who tries to stab you in the back. You get to them first."

"Shut up," Rosco hissed at her. "You do not know what you're talking about. Gareth is the liar!"

"No," Helen shook her head and held out a photograph. "You're the liar. You've been so jealous of Gareth, you tried to steal his life. The poor farmer's kid story. Falling for Rosie. Those were all Gary's memories, not yours. And then the worst is that you became a police officer so that you could hide your lies and bury Gary in a prison so deep he would forget the warmth of the sun."

"I just don't get why?" Gary said, his eyes imploring Rosco for some kind of explanation. "Why did you do this to us?"

"Because you had it all," Rosco exploded at him, his face an unrecognizable mask of hatred. "The friends. The teachers. The parents who loved you. The girl. I was sick of it."

"But why did you have to kill Rosie?" Gareth gushed, tears streaming down his cheeks. "You could've taken it out on me. Hurt me. But why take her beautiful life away?"

"Because she didn't want me!" Rosco roared. "Do you know how it feels to have everyone reject you because your idiot friend is just so much better? I mean, even Helen," Rosco stormed over to her, "she chose you after one conversation, when I've been working my case for weeks. You have ruined everything, and I'm going to make you pay for your terrible choice, just like I made Rosie pay."

"Rosco, no!" Gareth shouted.

Rosco yanked Helen up by the arm and pulled a small pistol out from his police jacket, sticking the end to her temple.

"Not so fast," Rosco warned with a malevolent smirk. "I wouldn't want to blow these pretty brains everywhere."

"You know I'm tiring of being kidnapped, held at gunpoint, and in need of being rescued," Helen stated with an exasperated sigh.

"Shut up!" Rosco roared in her ear. "This is how it's going to go, Gary. You're going to hand yourself in, confess to your murders and serve out the rest of your pathetic life in prison where you deserve to rot. If you promise to do all that, I'll let the woman live."

Gareth was crying again. Helen could not quite fathom how he was called Gareth the Grim.

"Alright," Gareth cried, slowly lifting his hands into the air. "I'll do as you wish. Just let her go."

Rosco frowned. "On second thought, I think a better plan would be to shoot you both and blame her murder on you. It worked the first time, after all."

"You bastard!" Gareth shouted.

"That's enough, Rosco," Noah announced as he stalked out from behind the shed. "We've got you surrounded, and we all heard your confession."

"Put your gun down," Ruby ordered as she stepped out with her weapon trained on Rosco.

Several other officers stepped out into the clearing, their guns glinting metallic in the fading moonlight.

"Stay back!" Rosco shrieked. "I'll take us both out."

Just then, Helen felt a familiar feeling as a body wove in between her ankles. A gruff meow alerted her to Agatha. All it took was one aggressive shake from Rosco to set the temperamental cat off.

Agatha latched onto his ankle with her longest canines and shredded his pants leg with ferocious claws. If that was not enough, the wicked cat flashed up his leg at lightning speed and under his shirt, where she delivered even more damage.

Rosco screamed, his focus shifting off his gun for the briefest second. This was enough for Boris to step up behind

Rosco and whack him over the head with a small marble statue.

"Frame me," Boris muttered as Rosco crumpled to the floor with a groan. "That will teach you to snoop around my office."

"Oh, Boris!" Helen cooed, wrapping her arms around his neck and hugging him. "You saved me!"

"For a price, of course," he teased.

Gareth was next to draw her into a hug.

"How can I ever thank you?"

"All I did was get caught in my trap," Helen laughed sheepishly. "I really need to take some defense classes or something."

"No, thank you for believing me when no one else would. You showed me more kindness, even though I was a complete stranger, than anyone has done in a long time," Gareth continued. "I am forever in your debt."

Chapter 11
Celebrations

The village overflowed with visitors over the next few days. Considering Rosco's arrest and Gareth's exoneration, the town extended the harvest festival, filling the streets with stalls, glowing lights, cheerful music, and tantalizing food.

Noah and Ruby's captain were so thrilled with the fame the high-profile case brought their little district that he immediately promoted them both. That meant they were no longer work partners and were free to date.

Helen had not seen them since. She was working hard to be content with the solitude singleness brought her. As she roamed the streets, tasting new foods and waving off unwanted attentions from local males, Helen smiled.

She had made new friends, tasted fresh adventures, and almost been murdered by an encounter with hurried love. She knew in her heart that she was not ready to choose anyone to replace Peter. As she danced with a stranger, laughing and skipping along to steps she did not know, and sipping beer and donning a wreath of wheat and field flowers, Helen accepted that just as there was beauty in being part of someone else, there was equal beauty in enjoying life to the fullest alone.

Helen pulled out of the dance, her partner quickly forgotten. She had seen someone. And it was not the dark flicker of a stranger on the edge of her vision. She knew this face, and he was smiling at her as he had for decades.

"What are you doing here?" Helen stammered, unsure of whether she could trust her eyes.

"Well," Alex smiled at her, his white-collared shirt still creased from the airplane, "I figured since you won't come home, I should join you."

Helen laughed. She flicked a wreath onto his head and handed him a beer.

"Why don't you just say it, Alex," she teased. "You missed me too."

The End

Now that you have finished this cozy mystery, please consider posting a review on Amazon. It would be appreciated.